JACKIE AND THE PONY CAMP SUMMER

D0733829

The Jackie Pony Series

Jackie and the
Pony Camp Summer

Judith M. Berrisford

**Hodder
Children's
Books**

a division of Hodder Headline plc

For Ian McNiellie, Chris Baker,
Stuart Dick, Raymond and Derek Jones

Copyright © 1968 Judith M Berrisford

First published in Great Britain
in 1968 by Brockhampton Press
This edition published in 1998 by Hodder Children's Books
A division of Hodder Headline plc
338 Euston Road
London NW1 3BH

10 9 8 7 6 5 4 3 2 1

A Catalogue record for this book is
available from the British Library

ISBN 0 340 57544 1

Printed and bound in Great Britain

Contents

CHAPTER ONE

NEW PONY FRIENDS

My cousin Babs and I halted our ponies as we reached the crest of the grassy hill. We looked towards a cluster of pink-washed farm buildings. A group of tents in a meadow beyond showed white against the fresh green of the headland which sloped to rocks and a sandy beach.

Sunlight gilded the tidepools, and foamy wavelets lapped against the sea's edge.

We turned our gaze back to the headland and the tents. So this was the Pony Camp where we were going to be helpers for the rest of the summer holidays.

'Where is everybody?' I said, because, at the moment, the camp seemed oddly deserted.

'They're probably all out on a picnic ride,' said Babs, touching Patch with her heels. 'Come on. Let's investigate.'

Soon we were dismounting in the cobbled stable-yard. I looked towards the empty stables.

'Hello!' I called. 'Anyone there?'

Just then a ginger head appeared through the open window of a hayloft, and a boy shouted: 'Shan't be a jiffy,' and immediately disappeared.

Then, strangely, only a few moments later, a ginger-haired boy in a yellow shirt and faded blue jeans strolled round the corner of the stables.

'Hi!' Babs called. 'I'm Babs Spencer, and this is my cousin, Jackie Hope.'

'And I'm Paul Wayne,' replied the boy. Then as we shook hands, we heard footsteps on some wooden stairs, and another ginger-haired boy appeared. I blinked in surprise, thinking that I was seeing double. Both boys were identical from their ginger heads, blue eyes and freckled faces to their yellow shirts and faded jeans.

'Twins,' exclaimed Babs. 'However are we going to tell you two apart?'

'Most people don't,' said the newcomer. 'I'm Pete and he's Paul.' He smiled. 'I like the look of your ponies.'

The twins made a fuss of Misty and Patch

before taking us to the stable near the loose-boxes to unhitch our kit and unsaddle our ponies. We left Misty and Patch pulling at hay nets in the sweet-smelling dimness. Beside them was another pony who, in the gloom, might easily have been mistaken for Patch although, on closer look, I saw that he was really black and white – a piebald – whereas Bab's Patch was skewbald – brown and white.

Pete – or was it Paul? – put his hand on the piebald's withers and fondly straightened his mane.

'This is Magpie,' he said. 'He's in here because he's waiting to have a shoe fixed. The other ponies are out on a ride with the campers. They'll all be back for high tea at six.'

'In the meantime,' said the other twin, 'we'll help you to put up your tent so that you can settle in. Then perhaps you can give us a hand to get a meal ready for the campers.'

We pitched our green ridge tent, put down the groundsheet and pumped up our air mattresses. Then, hanging our jackets from hooks on the tent pole, we rolled up our sleeves and followed the boys to a canvas shelter which was erected over a field kitchen.

While the boys kindled the fire and piled on

9

sawn-up branches, Babs and I examined the food store. There were big cans of soup, vast tins of baked beans, fruit, jam, and plenty of dehydrated mashed potatoes.

'What's for tea?' Babs asked.

'Sausages and chips – and that means peeling all these,' said Pete, dragging out a carton of potatoes.

Babs and I dipped the potatoes into a bucket of water and peeled while the boys sliced. By the time the campers returned, hot, tired and hungry, the fat was bubbling merrily, and an outsize basket of chips was beginning to brown.

Babs shook the chip basket from time to time, while I prodded the sausages in the large frying pan with a fork.

'Good work!' said an approving voice, and we looked up to see an auburn-haired young woman, of about twenty-one or so, the twins' sister, Sheila. She introduced us to the campers – five girls and four boys, aged from about eleven to sixteen.

After tea and washing up, in which the campers helped, Sheila and Pete took us to meet the rest of the ponies, while Paul held Magpie for the blacksmith who had just arrived.

'We've only got ten ponies at the moment,'

10

Sheila explained, leading the way to a field where all the ponies were turned out to graze.

'Plus Misty and Patch,' offered Babs. 'You can borrow them if you're short. How many campers are there going to be?'

'Well, let me see,' said Sheila. 'Eight are going home tomorrow, and another ten are arriving.'

'So you're really fully booked,' said Babs.

'Oh, no,' said Sheila. 'We can always put up more tents and get more ponies if other people want to come. The more the merrier.'

I looked across the paddock, beyond a drystone wall, where the Waynes' ponies were grazing.

They were mostly about fourteen hands high – two browns; a dun with the wild-horse black line down his back and with a long black tail; two roans – one strawberry and one blue; a chestnut with a bright mane and tail; a black; one bay with dark points, and one bay with a light mane and tail.

'Hey, Daydream.' Sheila gave a soft whistle, and the bay with dark points came trotting up to her. 'We usually keep her up because she's a show-jumper,' she told us. 'But she's out in the field today with the others for a change.'

11

'Sheila!' shouted one of the campers from the farmhouse doorway. 'Trunk call. A brother and sister from Epping want to book up for the week after next.'

She smiled at Babs and me. 'Business is getting brisk. You're bringing us luck. Something tells me we'll make a success of this Pony Camp.'

'Cross your fingers for luck!' I said quickly, and thought: you wouldn't have said that, Sheila, if you'd known what a pair of jinxes Babs and I are supposed to be.

CHAPTER TWO

THE DIFFICULT TWIN

I was still admiring the bay pony, who stood near me hoping for sugar, while Sheila hurried to answer the telephone.

'Daydream's a beauty,' I said to Pete, running my hand down her neck and patting her firm withers, while I admired her firm bone and springy hocks. 'I'd love to try her.'

'Well then, jump up,' said Pete. 'You won't need a saddle. She's perfectly quiet.'

I climbed on to Daydream's back from the wall and she moved off at once with an easy gait.

'Come on, girl.'

I touched her with my heels and she broke into a smooth trot. Then we cantered. Round the paddock she went, answering to my legs and to the touch of my hands on her neck.

'She's like a mind-reader,' I said, halting her

in front of Pete and Babs. 'She seems to know exactly what one wants her to do without any need for a bridle.'

'Yes, she's wonderful, isn't she?' Pete agreed, rubbing the bay pony affectionately between the eyes. 'Would you like to try her over a jump?'

'Could I?'

'I don't see why not,' said Pete. 'You managed her jolly well just now, and she's a willing jumper.'

'Lucky you,' Babs said to me enviously, as Pete went to the stables and came back a few moments later carrying a pole and two light-weight trestles which he fixed up to make a low cavaletti.

'There you are,' he said, stepping back. 'Instant obstacles. Try her over that, Jackie.'

Daydream gave an excited toss of the head when I rode her towards the cavaletti. It was obvious that she loved jumping. I touched her with my heels, and she broke into a canter. Steadily, with perfect timing, she approached the jump. She took off effortlessly and sailed over. She jumped like a dream, I thought. No wonder she was called Daydream.

I rode her round the field. Then I put her at the jump once more. Again she gave that pleased toss of the head. Neck extended, she approached the jump, tucked her forefeet well up, took off and was over.

'Well done,' called Babs, and Pete turned round the trestles to make the jump higher.

'Try that,' he urged.

As I approached the jump a whinny came from the stables, and there was a thud of hooves. I turned to see my pony, Misty, cantering towards the paddock.

'Look out,' Babs warned. 'Misty's jealous.'

I groaned. Misty must have heard us making a fuss of Daydream, and now, not wanting to be left out of anything, she was coming to see what was happening.

'Go back, Misty,' I called, halting Daydream and waving my pony away from the paddock. Babs scrambled over the wall and ran to catch her. Misty swung out of Bab's reach and jumped into the field.

Mischief in her eyes, my pony was coming straight for me and Daydream.

'Oh Misty, you bad pony,' I sighed, sliding off Daydream and running to catch Misty who brushed past me, knocking me sideways. Eyes rolling, she went up to Daydream, darted her neck forward and gave the bay a nip on the withers. Daydream backed, kicked and caught one of the other ponies. Pete ran to catch her, and the other ponies, startled, jostled together in a foot-stamping huddle at the far end.

'What's happening?' exclaimed a boy's voice, and we turned to see Paul staring at the milling group of ponies, while he hitched Magpie to the gate. 'For goodness' sake!' he groaned, running into the field. 'Grab that grey pony before she does any more damage. Pinky looks as if he's been lamed, and if any of the others get kicked they'll be out of action for a week, just when we need every pony for the campers.'

'Don't flap, Paul,' said his twin over his shoulder as he helped Babs and me to corner Misty. I grabbed Misty, and Pete turned to face Paul. 'Pinky isn't really lame,' he declared, running gentle hands down the strawberry roan's off-hind. 'It was only a brush.'

'All the same, it might have been serious,' Paul pointed out. 'Anyway, Pete, I think you ought to have known better than to let a strange girl ride Daydream bareback, and try to jump her. I thought we'd decided to put all the jumps away.' He turned to Babs and me. 'How did your pony get out of the stable? You can't have tied her up properly or shut the door.'

16

I felt guilty. I suppose we'd been so thrilled at arriving at the camp and seeing everybody that we'd given Misty a hay net and left her to it It was quite possible that we'd been too excited to tie her up securely or to shut the door, as Paul said.

'I'm sorry, Paul,' I said soberly. 'I suppose we have been careless.'

'And because of that,' Paul replied, 'a pony's been kicked. Well, you've been lucky. It might have been serious.' He moved across to Misty. 'This pony isn't to be trusted with the others yet awhile.' He turned to me. 'Is she always so vicious?'

'Misty hasn't an ounce of vice in her,' Babs said, rushing to my pony's defence. 'She's a sweet, good-tempered pony.'

'Good-tempered ponies don't bite,' Paul said. 'She'll have to be kept apart from the others until we see how she's going to settle down.'

We turned to Pete. What did he think? Would he back us up?

'Better do as Paul says, Jackie,' he said quietly.

Feeling deflated, Babs and I took Misty back to join Patch in the stables, while Paul walked towards the farmhouse followed by Pete.

'That's done it,' Babs said ruefully. 'We're in disgrace already. I suppose it was our fault, but, oh dear, I'll never understand why Paul got so cross when Pete didn't make any fuss at all.'

'I expect we deserve it,' I said sadly. 'We usually do.' I turned to my pony. 'Oh, Misty,' I scolded. 'You have been a bad pony letting us down like that just when Babs and I were trying to make a good impression.'

Misty rubbed her nose against my sleeve as if to tell me that she was sorry. With a sigh, I put her back into the stable. As she pulled at her hay, Babs and I walked back towards the house, still feeling downhearted.

'Not to worry!' Sheila greeted us. 'Mishaps will happen. I saw it all through the window.' She looked at dark clouds which were gathering in the evening sky. 'We're all going to the big barn for a pony quiz until the storm's over. You know a lot about ponies. So here's your chance to shine. Come on – cheer up.'

CHAPTER THREE

OTHER PEOPLE'S PONIES

Miracle of miracles! I won the pony quiz, and Babs came second. Sheila presented us with a pony book each as prizes, and we hoped that we were in favour again as one of the twins patted us on our backs in congratulation.

'Thanks, Paul,' I said.

'I'm Pete,' he told me with a friendly smile, and I looked across the barn with a sinking heart, to see that Paul's back was turned on us as he looked out of the window. Well, we'd just have to try harder and hope to earn his approval. It did seem strange that Pete was so kind and friendly, while Paul had quickly become grumpy and hostile as if he'd taken a dislike to me and Babs.

Just then Sheila began to play a jangly piano, and everyone started a sing-song.

An hour later, hoarse but happy, we joined

the other campers in a dash over the wet grass to our tents. We were asleep almost as soon as our heads touched the air pillows.

Next morning we were awakened by the sound of a hunting horn just outside our tent.

'Breakfast's ready,' Pete called. 'Come and get it.'

'Where have you two been?' demanded Paul, as Babs and I appeared after hurriedly scrambling into our clothes. 'Sheila could have done with your help in getting the breakfast. It's up early in the morning here, you know.'

'Sorry,' I said meekly. 'We'll be sure to be in time to help tomorrow.'

Sheila handed everyone large plates full of bacon, tomato, sausages and fried bread. 'We may only have time for a scratch lunch,' she told Babs and me. 'So eat plenty now. Then perhaps you'll lend a hand cleaning up the house.'

We were flipping round with dusters and mop when a telephone bell rang. Pete ran to answer it. 'Just a minute,' he said, in reply to an excited young voice over the line. 'I'll have to ask my sister.'

Putting his hand over the mouthpiece he called through the open window to Sheila who was in the yard checking Magpie's shoes. 'It's those three boys from Milltown. They're not going on their school trip to Paris after all. So they want to know if they can come here instead. Can they come today?'

Sheila thought for a moment, and then quickly made up her mind.

'Yes, we'll fit them in somehow,' she decided, and as Pete noted down the time that the boys would need picking up from the station with their kit, she said to us: 'Never turn customers away. That's rule number one for a successful business.'

'And rule number two,' said Paul, with a trace of grumpiness, 'is make sure that there is a pony for every camper before you accept more bookings.'

'I've thought of that,' Sheila said, undaunted. 'I've fixed up to borrow extra mounts from the Rivermouth Stables. We need someone to ride over to fetch them.' She turned to me. 'Would you like to go with Pete?'

I agreed readily.

'Well, my advice is: if you let Jackie go, don't let her take Misty,' advised Paul. 'That mare would probably bite the other ponies.'

I was about to stick up for Misty. Then I thought: what's the use? After all, Misty had been jealous of Daydream, and had definitely given her a nip, so Paul had a point there.

'Take my pony,' Babs offered.

As I saddled Patch, I had some misgivings. Somehow I felt nervous every time I thought of Paul, and that made me do things wrong. If only Paul could be identical with Pete in character, as well as in looks. Pete was so happy-go-lucky, and he obviously liked Babs and me.

I trotted Patch into the lane, humming to myself and trying to shake off my thoughts about the difficult twin. Pete recognized the tune and whistled in harmony as he jogged ahead of me on Daydream.

I rode close to the verge, keeping Patch well under control. Passing traffic came near, often fast, and I knew the risk of being absent-minded or scatter-brained at such times.

Coming back along the road would be the test, with our own two ponies and three strange ones as well. If anything went wrong, Paul would be sure to say: 'I told you so.'

'We're nearly there,' Pete called over his shoulder, cutting into my forebodings. 'First turning on the left.'

The Rivermouth Stables were grander than I had imagined. Purpose-built loose boxes lined an orderly stable-yard. Neat signs on the doors proclaimed TACK ROOM AND OFFICE.

Dismounting and tying Patch and Daydream to a hitching bar, Pete and I went to the door marked OFFICE, and knocked.

'Come in,' called a voice, and we walked in to find a youth of about nineteen blinking at us through heavy, horn-rimmed spectacles.

'Yes?' he queried, eyebrows raised.

'We've come for the ponies,' said Pete.

'Oh, have you?' the youth said, in surprise. 'I rather expected Miss Wayne to come in person. However – ' He took off his spectacles and tapped them on some papers in a self-important way '– perhaps you'd better read through this.'

He pushed forward a typewritten document. I peered over Pete's shoulder to read:

I hereby take delivery of the three under-mentioned ponies

Pixie – brown with white stockings on near-hind, and white hairs on withers, fourteen h.h.

Strawberry – roan with white blaze and black mane. Six years old, thirteen-three h.h.

23

Bobbin – bay with black points, fourteen-two h.h.

I certify that they were sound and in good condition on receipt; and that I will be fully responsible for returning them in the same condition on or before the fifth of next September, or whenever required to do so by their owner – H. Stanley Morrison, Rivermouth Stables, Ringbury.

Signed................

date

'Well, that's easy,' I said. 'Pete and I will sign it, and then we can take the ponies.'

'But you're both minors,' the youth pointed out, 'and this is a legally binding document and must be signed by someone over twenty-one. Those three ponies are worth a great deal of money.' He waved his spectacles at us. 'I'm sure you'll appreciate that my father has to have some safeguard.'

Pete looked crestfallen. 'I suppose so,' he said. 'But more campers are arriving today along with three boys who weren't expected until later. They'll all want to ride this afternoon. We need the ponies now.'

'I've got it!' I said. 'Pete is Sheila's brother, and the Pony Camp is a joint enterprise run by

24

the Wayne family. Let Pete sign and put on behalf of Sheila Wayne.'

The youth looked doubtful. 'It doesn't seem quite right to me. We've got to have a grown-up signature as well. Oh, very well.' He handed Pete a ball-point pen. 'Both of you sign one of these carbons and then I'll give you the top copy to take back to the camp. Please get Sheila to sign it, and see that it's posted back to us this afternoon. Okay?'

Pete and I followed the youth across the stable-yard to a range of looseboxes where the three ponies were waiting already saddled and bridled, their stirrup irons run up to the top of their leathers.

'Mount your own ponies,' suggested the youth, 'and then I'll hand you the reins of these when you're ready.'

With Pete leading Pixie and Strawberry, and me leading Bobbin, on our near sides, we walked our mounts through the gate and on to the road.

'What a lot of red tape!' said Pete, breaking into a trot. 'I thought we were never going to get the ponies.'

'And what a stuffy young man,' I echoed feelingly. 'He sounded more like eighty instead of eighteen.'

'He's got ambitions to be a lawyer,' said Pete, 'so that probably accounts for it. He's never been very horsy, either. All the same, I suppose one can't blame him for being fussy. These are valuable horses. Perhaps we'd better not take them on the main road. We can get back to camp via the country lanes, but it's two miles longer.'

'Better be slow than sorry,' I said, as we turned down a quiet road.

Strawberry and Pixie seemed to go quietly enough beside Daydream, though Bobbin was quite jumpy. He kept twitching a muscle on his flank, and giving a dancing step. He didn't really seem as calm as he should have done for a staid pony, guaranteed safe for beginners. However, I was not very worried. I felt that I could control him well enough from Patch's back.

Suddenly Bobbin shied at a paper bag in the hedge and cannoned into us, squashing my leg against Patch's side, and banging my knee on the saddle.

'Hey, look out,' I warned Bobbin. 'Ah well, I suppose I'd better ride you, and lead Patch.' I reined up and called: 'Wait a minute, Pete.'

I slid down from Patch's back and sorted out the reins before mounting Bobbin. Just then a motor scooter careered round the bend and raced noisily past.

Bobbin snorted and shied, dragging his reins from my fingers. He wheeled, plunged across the verge and jumped the hedge. There was a frightened squeal, and then he disappeared from view.

With a sick feeling in my tummy I scrambled up the hedge bank and looked over. There, in a deep hidden ditch, lay the pony, quite still.

Leading the other three ponies, Pete hurried to the bank.

'He isn't moving,' he reported. 'Here, hold these.'

He passed me the ponies' reins and clambered over the hedge as Strawberry, one of the other Rivermouth ponies, lifted her head and whinnied, sensing that something was wrong with her stable-mate.

The whinny seemed to bring Bobbin back to life. His sides heaved as he took a deep breath. Then he threshed his hooves, trying to roll over to get up, but his efforts seemed to make him slip farther into the muddy ditch. He slid on to his back and, still struggling, wedged himself tighter.

Pete scrambled down the bank. He stood ankle-deep in mud beside the threshing pony.

'Steady, Bobbin.' He grasped the pony's bridle and heaved to no avail. Bobbin still lay struggling. 'He'll burst his guts if we don't get him out soon.' Pete was getting desperate. 'What we need is a rope and a tractor. Tie the other ponies up, Jackie, and take Patch for help.'

I put a foot into Patch's stirrup ready to mount to ride to the nearest farm. Just then I heard the peep of a car horn, and an old taxi came round the bend with luggage strapped and roped to its roof-rack. I took my foot out of the stirrup and, pulling Patch behind me, ran across the verge and into the middle of the road, holding up my hand to flag the taxi to a halt.

The plump taxi-driver leaned anxiously out of the window. 'Anything wrong, love?'

'Plenty,' I said feelingly, and turned to see several boys and girls in the back. The girls were wearing jodhpurs. 'Pony people – thank heavens!' I gasped. 'I expect you're on the way to the Pony Camp. I'm a helper there. So please come to the rescue.'

'What's wrong?' asked one boy.

'It's a pony. He's stuck in a ditch on the other side of the hedge,' I explained. 'He's on his back, and if we don't get him out quickly he may rupture himself and have to be shot. We need ropes.'

'Quick!' Pete's desperate voice floated over the hedge. 'Hurry! I can't keep him still.'

CHAPTER FOUR

TRYING TO HELP

'Coming, sonny!' The fat taxi-driver lumbered breathlessly into the field while we tugged at the knots of the rope holding the luggage.

By now all the others were helping. We disentangled the ropes and straps, and buckled and knotted them in one strong length. My fingers fumbled as I slid the last buckle home. Then, carrying our improvised rope between us, we hurried into the field.

In the ditch, Pete and the taxi-driver were standing one on either side of Bobbin, encouraging him to keep still so that he would not strain himself.

We passed the 'rope' to Pete who fastened it to the front of Bobbin's running martingale which, luckily, was not broken. Then, leaving the taxi driver in the ditch to help the pony, the rest of us took up our position on the bank, holding the rope like a tug-of-war team. We pulled, but nothing happened.

'We're just not strong enough,' groaned one of the boys. 'It would take more than us to move that pony and get him back on his feet.'

One of the girls, who was called Wendy, looked round for inspiration, and her eyes caught the roof of the taxi. 'I know!' She scrambled down into the ditch to replace the taxi-driver at Bobbin's side. 'If you can bring the taxi into the field,' she told the plump man, 'we could fasten the rope to that.'

The driver backed his vehicle through the gate and over the grass.

'The bumper won't stand the strain, I reckon,' he grunted. He lowered himself on to the grass and wriggled on his back under the taxi to buckle one end of the rope round the axle-case. Then, puffing his way out with difficulty, he stood up and got into the driving seat to put the taxi into gear while we all stood ready to push, shove and hoist Bobbin to his feet.

The taxi's wheels spun before they gained a hold in the soft ground. The rope strained and the leather creaked. With a squelch of mud, Bobbin was pulled first to his knees, and then, lumberingly, to his feet. He stood trembling before scrambling out of the ditch.

'Hurrah!' panted Wendy, patting the frightened pony. 'I never thought we'd do it.'

Pete plucked handfuls of long grass from the hedge and, using them with his handkerchief, rubbed Bobbin down, while one of the girls removed his saddle.

'He's breaking into a sweat,' said Pete. 'Get some more grass, Jackie, and rub him down on the other side. He'll get a chill if we're not careful.'

Suddenly Bobbin's ears pricked, and he gave a neigh. An answering neigh from the gate made us look round to see a serious-looking man, with a moustache, dismounting from a chestnut horse.

'What's happened to Bobbin?' the man asked in a stern voice.

'Er, hullo, Mr Morrison,' gasped Pete, and we realized that this was Bobbin's owner and the father of the stuffy young man who was so legally minded.

'Nothing to worry about,' I told Mr Morrison in what I meant to be a reassuring voice. 'It's all over and no harm done.'

'The pony was in a proper fix, sir,' the taxi-driver said. 'But these youngsters did the right thing.'

I looked anxiously at Mr Morrison. He didn't

seem reassured by the taxi-driver's words. 'I don't want to make difficulties for you,' he said to Pete, 'but I've got to consider my ponies. They're my stock-in-trade. In fact my livelihood depends on them.' He took off his jacket and put it across Bobbin's loins. 'I can't risk letting you take him to your camp. He'll have to come back to my stables.'

'But, Mr Morrison – ' Pete protested and stopped as Mr Morrison turned away to look at Strawberry and Pixie who were standing by the hedge.

'I can't manage the three of them myself,' Mr Morrison said firmly. 'Perhaps two of you will be good enough to bring the other two ponies along for me.'

Pete stared at Mr Morrison in dismay. 'Please give us another chance and let us keep Strawberry and Pixie,' he begged. 'If you don't, we shall be short of ponies for the camp.'

'I couldn't risk it.' Mr Morrison shook his head. 'Sorry. Now be reasonable and don't let us have any argument about this.'

With heavy hearts, Pete and I mounted our ponies, and led Strawberry and Pixie behind Mr Morrison, back to his stables from which we had collected them an hour earlier. Meanwhile, the campers got back into the taxi which squelched out of the field and started on its way again towards the Pony Camp.

Pony Camp! I thought as its engine faded behind the clip-clop of our ponies' hooves. What kind of a Pony Camp would it be without the three extra ponies which Sheila had been counting on? What would she say when we got back and told our woeful news? Worse still, what would Paul say?

Of course Paul was furious –
I was sitting on my camp-bed, writing to Mummy and Daddy that evening.

And I must admit it's a bind because, with three ponies short, it means that Babs and I will have to lend Misty and Patch to the campers, and we and one of the twins will have to stay behind to do camp chores while the others go off for picnic rides. Sheila was disappointed, but she made the best of it, knowing that things always do go wrong from time to time wherever there are ponies.

But to get back to Pete and Paul. Considering that they're twins and look exactly alike, it's odd now different they are in character. Pete's always friendly and jolly and seems to take life as it comes and enjoys every moment, but Paul's somehow soured. If anything goes wrong he gets cross and always seems to blame it on Babs and me.

Babs wonders whether he's a girl-hater. But I don't know. He doesn't seem to like anybody. He gets a bit short with Pete, too. But Pete and Sheila just seem to accept his bad temper. You'd think they'd just tell him not to be so grumpy. But they never do. Perhaps they've tried, and found it makes him worse.

Meanwhile we're still in the middle of a pony flap — or should I say ponyless flap? Six more campers are due to arrive tomorrow and then we shall be nine ponies short. Sheila's been phoning round to all the other stables and she hasn't been able to get a single pony. The owner of one of the stables was quite nasty to her. It seems she'd heard about the mishap to Mr Morrison's Bobbin, and she wasn't risking anything like that happening to one of her mounts.

Well, more news, probably even more dire, in a few days.

Your loving daughter,
Jackie

The other six campers, four girls and two boys, arrived soon after tea next day. Babs and I helped them to put up two tents. Just as we were tightening the guy lines of the girls' tents, and showing them how to roll up the brailings, Pete sounded the hunting horn that the Waynes used to call the campers together.

We gathered round to see Sheila standing in the middle of the field, a sheet of paper in her hand.

'As you know, we're short of ponies,' she told the campers. 'So, until we get some more mounts, I'm going to divide you into two rides – A and B. Tomorrow, Ride A will go with Pete and myself for a picnic ride to Blueshell Bay, and Ride B, with Babs and Jackie and Paul, will visit the Home for Retired Horses at Birch Down. A minibus will call to take you there at 11 a.m.'

Babs and I looked at each other. The visit to the Home for Retired Horses would be super, but there had to be a snag. Why, oh why, had Sheila wished us on Paul, the grumpy twin?

'I suppose she thinks Paul may be able to keep us in order,' Babs sighed.

'Or she may want to give us the chance to

prove our pony-worth, and to redeem ourselves,' I said unhopefully. 'She's taking a chance.'

'We're jinxed when Paul's around,' Babs said feelingly.

Sure enough, next morning we were in the camp kitchen putting up the picnic lunches when Paul stormed in, and from that moment things started to go wrong again.

'Aren't those sandwiches cut yet?' he demanded, when he saw that Babs and I were still slicing up bridge rolls, and inserting the cheese and tomato filling. 'The minibus will be here in ten minutes.'

'Don't you fret. We'll be ready on time,' Babs assured him.

'Well, just see that you are,' said Paul, going off to round up campers.

Then we happened to turn our backs on the Primus for only a moment, to buckle up two rucksacks of food, and the milk boiled over. We had to sprinkle salt over the boiling-ring to take away the smell, and add a tin of condensed milk and a jugful of water to make up the loss.

Impatient horn toots from the minibus had already sounded before the milk had come to the boil. We were keeping everyone waiting.

All fingers and thumbs, Babs and I managed somehow to fill four giant Thermos flasks and screw down the tops before Paul stormed in again.

'Aren't you ready yet?' he demanded.

'Coming. Oh, just a minute,' gasped Babs. 'We've forgotten the cups.'

'And not only the cups, I bet.' Paul said with a groan. 'We'd better check. Now you look in the rucksacks, Jackie, as I call out the items. Spoons?'

I nodded meekly.

'Sugar?'

'Yes.'

'Biscuits? Sandwiches? Cake? Coffee?'

'Check,' I said, relieved and hopefully looked up for approval. 'Nothing missing.'

'Oh, come on,' said Paul, impatient. 'I've never met such a zany pair.'

I sighed and said nothing. Paul just didn't want to like us. It was impossible for me to do right. However, we must keep the peace for the sake of Sheila and Pete. Why did Paul have to be so *difficult*? Life at the Pony Camp would be wonderful if only Paul could be as pleasant as Pete.

And if wishes were ponies, all the campers would be riding. Life was never completely perfect, and people were never quite as one expected or hoped them to be.

With these philosophic thoughts, I silently took my seat beside Babs in the back of the minibus.

CHAPTER FIVE

A HORSY DAY

I wasn't downhearted for long. The driver of the minibus was something of a comic turn. He had long curly hair and side-whiskers. He fancied himself as something of a pop singer, so the minibus echoed as he gave us his version of several hits.

We all joined in, except Paul, and it was a jolly party that alighted in the white-railed enclosure in front of a rose-covered farm which was the headquarters of Birch Down Home for Retired Horses.

Mrs Green, who was in charge, led us into a big field. There, standing nose-to-tail, under the the shade of a chestnut tree, was a group of retired horses. They broke off their dozing and fly-swishing and cantered across as Mrs Green called them. Another horse lifted his head from the stream where he had been drinking, and trotted over. More came from over the brow of the hill, and soon we were surrounded by old, but healthy-looking, and obviously happy, horses. They ranged in size from a big Clydesdale, with shaggy legs, big hooves and gentle eyes, to a white donkey who had mothered many foals and had finally been rescued from a fairground in her thirtieth year.

There were also two cobs from a scrap merchant, a retired race-horse, three pit ponies, four farm horses and three Fell ponies.

'Bess and Amber and Brownie aren't really old enough to be retired,' Mrs Green told us, patting the Fell ponies as they nuzzled her sleeve, 'but they belonged to a gentleman who directed, in his will, that he didn't want his ponies to be sold from pillar to post. They were in danger of being put down, so we were able to persuade the executor to let them come here.'

Mrs Green left us to go back indoors where she had letters to write. We wandered over the fields, and ate our picnic by the stream. We were feeding scraps to the retired horses when a cattle van rolled up, and stopped before the farm.

Interested, we went across to see what

might be in the van. As we reached the white rails of the farmyard, Mrs Green came through the front door.

'This will be Magic Moment, our latest rescue,' she told us. 'Come and see.'

We crowded round as the ramp was let down and we could see, in the dimness of the van, fetlock deep in straw, a tall grey horse. The light seemed to dazzle him for a moment, and he made no attempt to move.

'Come on, then,' Mrs Green coaxed, going into the van. She grasped his head-collar and led him down the ramp. 'It's all right. This is your new home.'

Magic Moment stood uncertainly while Mrs Green made a fuss of him. We scrambled under the rail to add our welcome. Then Paul grabbed my shoulder.

'Keep back,' he warned. 'Can't you see he's a thoroughbred? You'll upset him.'

'Actually he's three-quarter bred,' said Mrs Green, trying not to be surprised by Paul's outburst. 'And you're quite right, Paul. Perhaps it's best not to overwhelm him too soon. He's a hunt horse.'

'I suppose he was going to kennels to make meat for the hounds,' Babs said, shocked. 'How wicked.'

'Yes, that's how it was,' Mrs Green said quietly. 'We had a hard job to persuade the hunt committee to let us buy him, and he was quite expensive. Still, he's safe now. Let's see how he takes to his companions.'

She led Magic Moment into the field. He caught sight of the other horses, and neighed. Captain, the Clydesdale, who seemed to be the leader of the retired horses neighed back, and, ears sideways, advanced to challenge the newcomer.

We all held our breath while the two horses suspiciously walked towards each other. Magic Moment's ears were lying flat and this was a tense moment. One never knew just what would happen when strange horses were introduced to each other.

'Quiet, everyone,' warned Paul.

We watched anxiously as Captain scraped the ground with an off-fore. Magic Moment did the same. Heads lowered and quite close together, ears all ways, the two horses repeated this procedure several times. Then, Captain turned and walked back to the other horses with Magic Moment following. Apparently the introduction had been successfully performed. To our relief, all the horses, led by Captain, raced round the field, tails streaming, their coats glistening in the sunshine. The white donkey brought up the rear. Magic Moment had been accepted by the herd.

'Lovely,' said our pop-singer driver. 'This calls for a whip-round.' He produced 50p. 'Put that towards buying the next horse,' he told our hostess. 'Fancy folk making nice horses into dog's meat, and after they've served them faithfully, too. Heartless, some people are.'

We all felt in our pockets and added what spare money we could find.

'Five pounds, eighty-three pence,' said Mrs Green gratefully. 'I must give you a receipt, and I'll put this into the Buying Warboy Fund. Warboy's the next hunt horse that we're bidding for.'

'Five pounds eighty-three won't go far towards buying a horse,' Babs said. 'Still, I suppose it's a start . . . I know!' Her face lit up. 'I've just had an idea.' She turned to Mrs Green. 'You know that you said Bess and Amber and Brownie weren't really old enough to be retired?'

I crossed my fingers and looked at Paul who was frowning. No doubt he could guess what was coming next.

'Yes, dear,' Mrs Green said encouragingly.

'Well,' went on Babs, 'do you think they'd

enjoy doing a bit of light work in a really happy home for the next few weeks? The money that they earn could go to buying Warboy.'

'And it would be doing us and the Pony Camp a good turn,' I added, not daring to look at Paul.

'Would it?' asked Paul, his blue eyes smouldering. 'Well, you might have asked me what I thought about it.'

Mrs Green turned to him with a helpful smile. 'Yes, I'm sure Bess and Amber and Brownie would be all right with you. I know Sheila's very good with ponies; and I think Mr Danesbury would have approved. After all, they're not really going from pillar to post. They'll be back here in a month, and the change might do them good. They're young enough to enjoy a few outings, and they would be helping to pay for Warboy. What do you think, Paul?'

Paul was still frowning. He looked from Babs to me, and then across at Mrs Green.

'I think it's quite a good idea, Mrs Green,' he said with an effort. 'Thank you very much.'

'No need for you to hurry the ponies back to camp,' said Roger, the oldest of the other campers, as Paul, Babs and I went with Mrs Green to collect the Fell ponies' tack. 'We'll

45

be back long before you, so we'll be able to start getting the meal.'

'Yes, that would be fun,' said Wendy. 'I've longed to try my hand at camp cooking ever since I arrived. Just tell us what is on the menu.'

'We were planning to have chops, tomatoes and fried potatoes,' said Babs, 'but if you can't manage that, use one of the big tins of corned beef and make a salad.'

The campers rolled off in the minibus and we heard their voices, led by the young driver, float back in song through the open windows.

With Babs mounted on Brownie, Paul on Bess and me on Amber, we thanked Mrs Green and rode out of the main gate.

Amber played up right away. The excitement of leaving the farm and seeing the big world again went to her head, and she progressed sideways for the first half-mile. Then a car whooshed past and she tried to climb the hedge-bank.

'There, silly.' Shortening my reins, I put my hand on her neck to reassure her.

'You managed that quite well, Jackie,' Paul said, appreciative for once, and I felt overwhelmed. He was actually making an effort to be pleasant to me. Wonders never cease.

The road forked. The main road with its stream of holiday traffic led back to Sandbeach. The other route was a bridle path dwindling into a sandy track behind the dunes and over the rim of the downs.

'We'd better go this way,' said Paul. 'Then Amber won't have any traffic to upset her.'

Paul opened a gate, holding it while Babs and I rode through. Babs caught my gaze, and gave a pleased wink and a nod. I knew what she was thinking. Was Paul trying to be gallant, polite and friendly? Had we won him over after all?

We trotted along the sandy track, with an occasional sideways dance from Amber. Then we came to the downs, and the mare gave a buck as she felt the turf under her hooves. She was fighting the bit, eager to be off. I decided to let her gallop to take the tickle out of her feet.

Amber extended herself, her hooves thudding and flecks of foam appearing on her neck. I let her gallop up the hill, and then pulled her up. Now she was resigned to a walk.

I turned in the saddle; Babs and Paul were some way behind. They seemed only to be trotting, so I walked Amber slowly on and then reined up, waiting for them to draw level. Suddenly, down on the beach below, a line of riders came into view round the sandhills. They were our pony campers, returning from their picnic ride with Sheila and Pete.

Pete was riding Daydream, and, as I watched, he pulled the bay mare away from the others and cantered purposefully towards a row of breakwaters. He took them stylishly, one after the other, the bay rising effortlessly.

'Look,' I said as Babs and Paul came up. 'Perfect timing. Pete certainly can jump.'

Babs shared my enthusiasm, but Paul barely glanced towards his twin. Annoyance showed in his face as he said to me: 'You are a clot, galloping off like that, Jackie. Amber was too fresh.'

'I thought it would be best to let her work off her excitement,' I tried to explain, but Paul cut me short.

'You were galloping wildly, out of control. Amber might have put her foot in a rabbit hole and broken her neck. Besides, your gallop might have upset Bess and Brownie, and started them playing up.'

I bit back a retort. It was no use arguing with him. He was his old grumpy self again. Silently I looked at him.

Paul's good-looking features were marred by anger. He was glowering towards the beach where his twin, having turned Daydream, was now riding back again over the breakwaters.

Paul dropped his gaze away as though for some reason he could not bear to look.

'What's wrong, Paul?' asked Babs in her most sympathetic tone. 'I know you're not upset simply because Jackie galloped Amber. There's some other reason. What is it? You can tell us.'

'Oh, shut up!' Paul's voice was taut. He spun his pony round. Then he said in a strangled tone, 'Come on. Let's get back to the camp now. And remember – no more galloping!'

CHAPTER SIX

THE HIDDEN TRUTH

'Just listen to the rain,' said Babs as we lay in our sleeping-bags under canvas that night.

Patter – patter – patter.

'A belt of heavy rain will sweep across Britain from the west particularly affecting coastal areas,' I quoted the weather forecast that we had heard on Roger's transistor during supper. 'Thank you and *good night*!'

We snuggled down, and I fell asleep to be wakened some hours later by Babs tugging at my shoulder.

'Something's happening,' said Babs. 'Listen.'

Above the sound of the downpour we heard voices. There was the flash of torchlights, and someone called:

'We're flooded out, too.'

50

'Trouble!' sighed Babs as we dressed and put on macs and wellingtons. 'I wonder whether Paul will blame us for this.'

Sheila and the twins were already coping with the emergency. Two tents were standing in several inches of boggy water, and the groundsheets were afloat in one of them, while a tin of talc was drifting down the field in a rivulet of muddy water.

'You can't stay here,' Sheila told the rained-out campers. 'Come across to the house, and we'll dry you out, and make up a couple of beds. Pete and Paul and Babs and Jackie will bring your kit.'

She shone her torch round at the other campers. 'Is anybody else's tent flooded?'

'Ours is worse than this one,' said a mousy-haired boy with spectacles.

'Then you'd better come across to the house, too,' said Sheila. 'How many are there of you, Micky? Six?'

Sheila led the flood victims to the farm, while the twins, Babs and I, equipped with torches, floundered through the muddy dark, salvaging the campers' belongings.

Soon after dawn, the twins, with the help of the boy campers, re-pitched the tents higher up the field. Then they all grabbed spades, and working in a row, sliced a ditch out of the muddy ground to drain away the water.

After lunch the rain became torrential.

Babs and I looked helplessly at Sheila. 'What are we going to do with the campers?' Babs asked.

'Well, this afternoon's taken care of,' Sheila told us, 'because Major Johnson, of the Pony Club, has promised to bring across his screen and projector and show some pony films.'

'What about tonight?' I asked.

'That's where you two can help,' said Sheila. 'Pete and Paul have got a portable cassette player, so I thought we might have dancing in the barn. I wonder if you could jolly it up a bit, put up some decorations and make it look festive.'

'Cross stirrups and stable brooms,' enthused Babs, catching on to the idea. 'Leave it to us, Sheila. We'll have a ball.'

Just then Sheila caught sight of Major Johnson's estate car through the window. 'I'll have to go and welcome our speaker now. You'll find some string in the top drawer of the dresser, and I think there are some old Christmas decorations in the corner cupboard.'

Leaving the campers to enjoy the pony films,

Babs and I raced off to the stables and, borrowing a couple of brooms, began to sweep out the barn with a will. We'd make this a dance to be remembered. Sweeping finished, we fixed a crossed broom and stable rake above the door, and another in the middle of the far wall. Then we tacked up stirrup irons to form a horseshoe with a broom and rake at the top. Underneath we placed an upturned stable barrow to serve as a table for the music, and flanked it with water buckets upside down.

We used half-full hay nets and well-polished bridles to decorate the side walls, and we dragged out the old piano, too.

'Now for the old Christmas decorations,' said Babs, starting off towards the farmhouse kitchen. 'I hope there are some streamers.'

Brushing the raindrops from our macs, we went into the kitchen. The whirr of the projector in the living room, and Major Johnson's voice explaining the forward seat, made a background with the rattle of rain against the window panes as we opened the corner cupboard.

'Oh, good – red and green streamers.' Babs's eyes lit up as she hauled them out. 'Cotton wool snowballs – no, they're too wintry. But those artificial fir branches will do nicely. Now for some string.'

I pulled open the drawer of the dresser. My gaze fell on a pile of gymkhana rosettes – ten or twelve red bearing the legend FIRST PRIZE, three or four blue, and one yellow.

'Just the thing.' I lifted them out. 'We can nail these on the rafters. They'll give a real pony atmosphere. Wait a minute.' I jerked the drawer forward. 'There are some more here.'

Two of the rosettes were wedged in the drawer at the back, so I lifted it out. As I did so the door of the cupboard underneath swung open and I caught a glimpse of a large silver cup.

'Goodness!' Babs pushed past me to inspect the trophy. 'If we polish this up, it'll look super. It's simply enormous. We might fill it with fruit cup.'

There were also some smaller cups. We lifted them out and placed them on top of the dresser, while we searched in various drawers for dusters and silver polish. They would make a wonderful set-piece for the pony dance.

'Fancy the Waynes winning all these,' I said, 'and not telling any of us.'

'These trophies definitely ought to be on display,' said Babs. 'They'd be a good advertisement for the Pony Camp.'

Suddenly I felt a draught on the back of my neck. I turned from the sink drawer where I had found the silver polish, and saw one of the twins standing in the doorway watching us.

Pete or Paul?

'What do you think you're doing?' The boy's eyes flashed as he glared from us to the cups and rosettes. Paul! 'Prying into our belongings, I see.'

'Hey, take it easy, Paul,' I protested. 'We're only looking for things to decorate the barn for the dance.'

'And these cups and rosettes are just the thing,' added Babs.

'Put them all back,' Paul ordered, and he looked so angry that I could picture him throwing them through the window.

'What's wrong?' I asked. 'Sheila told us to look for decorations for the dance, and these are absolutely super. Why hide them away? I should have thought you'd have been proud for people to see them. I would if I'd won all those.'

'So might I, if I had won them,' said Paul bitterly. He turned away, adding testily: 'Not that it's any business of yours.' He paused, and then said over his shoulder. 'Oh well, you may as well go ahead and use them. I can't stop you now.'

As Paul stalked away, Babs and I examined the cups.

PETER WAYNE
Under-16 Jumping – Open Championship Event
Fairlea Country Show

We looked from the big cup to the smaller ones. Peter Wayne Junior Jumping Competition. Peter Wayne under-14 pony trials. Peter Wayne under-16 one-day event.

'These are all Pete's,' I said, in surprise. 'None of them were won by Paul, nor even by Sheila. And I bet Pete won all those rosettes, too.'

Babs nodded. 'He was jumping marvellously over those breakwaters when we saw him on the beach yesterday.' She broke off, her eyes wide as at last she understood. 'So that's why Paul is so difficult. He's jealous of his twin – stark, staring *jealous*!'

CHAPTER SEVEN

SHOW-DOWN

Yes, Paul was jealous. I could see it all now. He couldn't bear the sight of other people being jumpers. That was why he'd been so angry when Pete had let me jump Daydream bareback, and why he'd been enraged at the sight of Pete jumping the breakwaters.

Babs and I voiced our thoughts as we got the refreshments ready for the barn dance.

'Pete and Sheila must have put the cups out of sight,' said Babs. 'I bet they thought it would be tactless to have them on display.'

'Gosh, yes!' I said, and added in alarm: 'And now Pete's cups are going to be on show tonight for everyone to see. I don't think we ought to have set them out.'

'Paul said we could,' said Babs.

'Yes, I know. But anyone could see that he really hated the idea.'

'Well, we can't put them back in the cupboard now without everyone asking a lot of questions,' said Babs. 'And then Paul will feel even worse.'

We speared sticks into some chippolata sausages. 'Somehow, Babs,' I said forebodingly, 'you and I just can't do right. There'll be ructions tonight over those cups, I know it.'

'How do you like Pete's pots. Jolly good, aren't they?'

I could hardly believe my ears. Those words were actually being spoken by Paul – the so-called jealous twin. He was standing by the display on a long table in the barn and speaking to the pony campers as they flocked in for the dance.

I listened in amazement.

Then I realized that Paul's words sounded carefully rehearsed. He was trying to be a good sport, trying to hide his jealousy. His smile was stiff, and his manner tense.

Just then Pete came into the barn, and Paul seemed to fade right into the background.

'Congrats, Pete,' said one of the girl campers named Cilla.

58

'A real show-jumper amongst us – what a thrill,' said the girl named Wendy. 'And we never knew.'

'What about entering for the Springfield Show, Pete?' put in Roger.

'I think you'll be in the White City class one day, Pete,' said another boy. 'How about giving me your autograph?'

Pete smiled, and chatted about his jumping triumphs, but I could see he was looking uneasy. After a moment he glanced round the barn for his twin. Then his smile faded. I followed his gaze and saw Paul, shoulders hunched, leaving the barn.

I felt so sorry for Paul. He'd made a big effort to be a good sport. Only Babs and I knew how hard he had tried to keep it up. Then, seeing everyone hero-worshipping Pete was too much for him. To show-jump must have been Paul's most cherished ambition; and he had probably found he was a duffer at it, while Pete was brilliant. That must have been a dreadful disappointment – and it had sown the seeds for his growing jealousy. If only I could help him.

'Come on, Jackie – dance!' Mickey's voice broke into my thoughts, and as we danced, my anxiety for Paul faded into the background for a while.

Then, three dances later, Babs grabbed my arm to remind me of a pony job that we had to do. Magpie had caught a chill, and just before the dance we had mixed him a bran-mash. Now was the time to give it to him.

As we hurried from the barn, I was reminded of Paul's earlier departure, and I looked around. I couldn't see him among the dancers. So he hadn't come back. What was he doing? Brooding, all alone in his room? Couldn't anyone do *anything* to make him feel happier?

Then Babs's voice dragged me back to the job in hand.

'It's just right,' she announced, removing the sacks from the bucket of mash. 'The mash has kept warm, but it's not too hot. Magpie's going to love this.'

We carried the bucket to the piebald's loose-box. The pony was standing there, sorry for himself. His ears pricked when he heard the clatter of a bucket, and soon he was lipping up the tasty mash.

Babs and I stayed with him until he had finished eating and started to doze. Then we crept out, closing the loosebox door. Strains of music wafted across to us from the barn.

'My favourite song,' said Babs, hurrying. 'Come on.'

'Just a minute.' I paused, suddenly feeling that something was missing from my wrist. 'My watch has gone. I'd better go back and look for it.'

'Don't be long,' said Babs, still heading for the barn. 'See you.'

I shone my torch down on to the floor of the loosebox, taking care to keep it out of Magpie's eyes, and searched among the straw for my watch. There it was, just beside the water bucket. I picked it up. The strap had broken. I put it in my pocket and was about to slip quietly out again without disturbing Magpie when I realized that I was not alone in the stables. There was somebody else – in Daydream's box at the far end of the range.

A boy's voice was talking softly to Pete's mare.

'Oh, Daydream! What am I going to do?'

I stiffened, recognizing the voice as Paul's. So he must have been in the stables all the time that Babs and I were feeding Magpie. He'd lain low so he wouldn't have to be pestered by us. Then, because he thought he was alone once more, he was pouring out his heart to the pony.

'Pete's a fine jumper,' Paul was saying. 'And here I am a real coward over jumping.'

He broke off. What was he doing now? Patting the pony, pressing his cheek against her neck?

I held my breath. Paul was speaking again

'I wish I could jump you, Daydream. That would be like the old days, wouldn't it, girl? We had good times together, you and I, until – '

I put my fingers in my ears. Paul was pouring out his heart, telling Daydream all the things he couldn't tell to anyone else. And I was having to eavesdrop. Worse still – I was going to sneeze! The dust from the straw was tickling my nose.

I put a finger along my upper lip trying to ward off the sneeze – and I had to hear Paul again.

'Well, I've got it off my chest.' Paul's tone now sounded more cheerful – more like Pete's voice. 'I've made up my mind. I'll show Sheila and Pete that I'm not jealous. I'll tell Pete he must go in for the Springfield Show – and I jolly well hope he gets some more pots.'

The sneeze was building up. I fought to suppress it. I was winning. The moment of danger was over. I relaxed and breathed again. Then – 'Atishoo!'

'What's that?' Paul's voice was edgy as he came into Magpie's box. 'Who's there?' His torch shone full on me as I tried to rush from the stables. 'Jackie!' Paul threw himself against the stable door, barring my escape. 'What are you doing here? You came back to hear what I was saying.'

'No, Paul, no.' I gasped. 'It's not like that. Really it isn't. Do let me explain. I dropped my watch and came back for it. Yes, I did hear what you said to Daydream. I understand everything now. Let me help.'

'Help?' Paul echoed. 'An interfering, scatter-brained girl like you? You and your nit-witted cousin! You're a pair of pests. I'm fed up to the teeth with you. Go on. Get back to the dance.'

He flung the door open.

'I'm not going,' I said 'until you've heard what I've got to say. I know why you're being angry with me. But I'm glad I overheard you, because now I understand. And I think it's terrible that you've got no one except Daydream to tell your troubles to.'

Paul's eyes smouldered. 'Are you going to go, Jackie, or do I have to throw you out?'

'Please listen, Paul,' I begged. 'You told Daydream that you weren't going to be jealous any more. Don't go back on that. I couldn't help hearing what you said, but I promise I won't breathe a word to anybody. Not even to Babs.'

'I don't care who you tell,' Paul challenged.

'Oh, yes, you do. You'd hate it. You feel humiliated because I heard what you said to Daydream. That's why you're so angry now. And I think it's such a shame – just when you'd made up your mind you were going to overcome your jealousy and help Pete to bring credit to the Pony Camp.'

'Shut up!' Paul's voice was curt. 'I don't want to hear.'

'I dare say,' I insisted. 'People don't like to face up to the truth. Yet you faced up to it when you were talking to Daydream. Why slip back? It was horrible for you that I should overhear it all, but it's not the end of the world. Lots of brothers get jealous of each other. Sisters, too – and cousins. Look, I *understand*. I don't blame you. You probably had some bad luck that spoilt your jumping chances. Why don't you tell me all about it? You might feel better then.'

'You'd be the last person I'd tell anything to.' Paul's voice was cold. 'Do I have to spell it out to you, Jackie? You're a P-E-S-T – a prying meddling *pest*. And so is your cousin. The best turn you could do me would be for you and Babs to pack up your kit and go. Go on! Get out! Out of this stable, and out of the Camp!'

CHAPTER EIGHT

A NOTE FROM PAUL

I fled from the sound of Paul's angry voice. I didn't go back to the dance in the barn. I couldn't face the lights and the music and the carefree dancers. I felt miserable as I ran to the camping meadow.

In the gloom of the tent I threw myself on the air mattress and sobbed. Everything had gone wrong. I'd failed. Instead of helping Paul, I'd humiliated him; and now he didn't want to see Babs or me again. We'd have to leave the camp. It would be impossible to stay here with Paul hating us, and to know that every time he saw us his pride would be hurt afresh.

If I'd been in his shoes I'd have felt the same. This was dreadful. I couldn't unburden myself, not even to Babs. So when she came back to the tent I pretended to be asleep. Then, when Babs asked, 'Are you asleep, Jackie?' I couldn't keep up the pretence and I blurted out: 'Oh, Babs, something terrible's happened. I can't explain. I promised not to. The fact is: we can't stay here any longer. We've got to go tomorrow.'

'It's something to do with Paul, isn't it?' Babs quickly sensed the truth. 'You've been crying. Has he been horrid to you? Why should we take any notice of him? We can't just go. We should be letting Pete and Sheila down. It's stupid?'

'Stupid or not,' I said unhappily, 'we can't stay here.'

Babs and I argued late into the night. She couldn't understand why I couldn't explain. We'd never had secrets before. She thought I ought to tell her, to trust her.

I suppose we fell asleep while we were still arguing, because suddenly it was morning and sunlight was glowing through the canvas.

I looked at my watch. Half-past six.

'Come on!' I shook Babs awake. 'We're making an early start. We've got to pack our kit, get Misty and Patch, leave a note and ride home.'

'Oh, go back to sleep,' groaned Babs.

I sat on my cousin's sleeping-bag, and grasped her by the shoulders. 'Now listen,

Babs – ' I would have to tell her everything after all. Then I broke off, listening. I could hear the swish-swish of gumboots in the dew-wet grass. Somebody was coming towards the tent. A shadow loomed over the canvas.

I held my breath, and signalled to Babs not to say anything.

'Jackie!' I heard Paul's voice from outside. 'Are you awake?'

I tried to make my voice steady as I said: 'What do you want?'

'Read this,' said Paul in a strained tone.

Paul's hand was thrust under the flap and I took a piece of paper from him.

As I opened the note I heard the thud-thud of his departing footsteps.

'What's it say?' Wide-awake now, Babs craned forward. We blinked and read:

You needn't go. It wouldn't solve anything. Pete and Sheila would only want to know what had happened, and so would the campers. It would lead to a lot of questions and fuss. Besides, we need your two ponies. If they went we'd be two mounts short. So you'd better stay after all, but please, Jackie, stop interfering and let me have a bit of peace. I've got to work things out for myself in my own way, and I can only do that if you and Babs keep out of my hair.

Paul

'Well, that's a relief – our not having to go after all,' said Babs. 'All the same, I think it's a cheek. Paul wants us to stay because it would make things awkward if we went. Yet at the same time he's telling us to keep out of his way. He hasn't considered our feelings, has he?'

I sighed. I didn't want to condemn Paul. We didn't know all the circumstances. Sheila and Pete hadn't told us, and why should they? It seemed that it was none of our business. All the same, when someone was unhappy and beset with problems as Paul was, I couldn't help feeling that someone had to do *something* to help. If only we *knew* more so that we could understand, and try once more.

'Oh, stop brooding about Paul.' Babs broke into my thoughts. 'There are other people in this camp, you know.'

Be busy – that was the way to stop brooding I thought, and there was certainly plenty to do. We cooked breakfast, packed the lunch rucksacks, and helped the campers brush their mounts, pick out hooves and saddle up. Misty gave me a puzzled look when Cilla rode her through the farm gate. With Magpie out of action, there wasn't a mount for either of the twins, and so they had to be left behind with us while Sheila rode Daydream.

'Come on,' Pete said as the hoof-beats died away. 'Let's see to Magpie and square up the camp. Then we can follow them. We've got four bikes.'

Magpie still had a cough. We gave him plenty of fresh water, greens and hay, deciding that Sheila would no doubt steam him that evening if necessary.

'You just snooze quietly, Magpie,' I told him, shutting the loosebox door. I was uneasy about leaving him, but I told myself that there wasn't much that we could do for him if we stayed.

Babs and I cut up the sandwiches for the boys and ourselves, and I was rather surprised that Paul had decided to come with us. He mumbled 'thank you' as I handed him his rucksack. Then he streaked off on his bike way ahead of us.

Even Paul's grouchiness could not dampen our spirits. Pete was his usual cheery self, and Babs and I felt our hearts lighten as we freewheeled down the winding hill from the headland. Paul was out of sight and out of mind for the moment.

We threaded through the Sandbeach traffic. Just ahead of us trotted a procession of donkeys, bells jingling, on their way to the sands.

The tide was on the ebb, and there was a splash of paddlers at the sea's edge. Passing the donkeys, we left Sandbeach and the promenade and turned along a honeysuckle-scented lane that led to Newberry Warren, with its bird sanctuary and forestry plantation of young trees.

We were on our way to Shell Island, an islet that was linked at low tide by a causeway to the mainland. As we breasted the hill, we could see it ahead of us beyond sandhills, rocky coves and a white-washed 'pepper-pot' of a disused lighthouse. The road led to a track through the dunes that had been planted with stands of young firs. Soon we had to dismount at a padlocked gate.

'We'll soon be there,' said Pete, gallantly lifting our bikes over the gate. 'You're going to like Shell Island. It's a real paradise.'

Small blue and brown butterflies flitted among the sandhills, and bees hummed among the tall, bright blue flower spikes of the wild anchusa that grew in clumps beside the track. We passed stands of fire-beating shovels, and Pete pointed out to us a watch-tower, built on stilts and roofed with pine branches. It was a lookout from which the forestry patrol could watch over the acres of young trees, and so instantly notice any outbreaks of fire caused by careless smokers or picnickers or, for instance, by broken glass intensifying the sun's heat and setting fire to dried wood.

'Oh, look!' I exclaimed when a biggish bird with long down-curved beak flew from the marram grass ahead of us, trailing its wing. 'A curlew. Poor thing, it must be hurt.'

'That bird's only pretending to be hurt,' said Pete. 'It's trying to fool us.' We stopped to watch the curlew flutter a little way ahead, and then droop its wing. 'Its nest must be near and it's trying to lure us away from the chick curlews.'

We trundled our bicycles along the track, enjoying the sweet scent of the yellow tree lupins that had been planted, with sea buck-thorn and dwarf willow, to bind the dunes so that the sand would not blow away during gales. At the side of the track, tiny wild pansies, purple and white and gold, starred the sand.

Soon we came to the causeway, a stony

embankment, seaweed-strewn and mussel-encrusted. It stretched for a quarter of a mile from the shore to Shell Island.

We shielded our eyes from the sun-glare and watched some black-headed sandwich terns swooping, fork-tailed and swallow-like, to dive into the sea after fish.

We crossed the causeway and felt a thrill as we stepped on to Shell Island, with its beach blue-tinged by the crushed shells of mussels. Treading short turf spangled with the magenta of wild geraniums, we reached the top of the island. A gentle ridge with rocky coves sloped to tidepools. On our left lay a row of whitewashed coastguard cottages and the old lighthouse.

The Wayne ponies, now unsaddled, were tied to the fence in front of the cottages, and we could see the campers splashing and swimming in the bay. I saw a red-headed boy among the swimmers – Paul. He was doing a good crawl stroke, and I felt pleased because, for once, he looked as though he was enjoying himself.

Leaving our bicycles by the coastguard cottages, we ran to the beach, changed into our swimsuits behind some rocks, and were soon splashing with the others in the sea.

After our bathe we let the ponies graze, keeping a watchful eye on them while we ate our picnic lunch. Then we split up to explore the island.

'Come back here, everybody, when you hear three blasts on the whistle,' said Sheila. 'We must leave here at two thirty sharp because of the tide. So be sure to listen for the whistle.'

CHAPTER NINE

DANGER ON SHELL ISLAND

Babs and I scrambled over the rocks. We discovered an old wreck in one of the coves, and picked sea-thrift that grew above the tideline. Then we sunbathed on one of the headlands, watching the waves lapping over the sand.

We must have dozed off because it seemed no time at all until we heard the whistle blast calling us back to the mainland. Everybody else had already assembled as we hurried towards the coastguard cottages, and Sheila was glancing anxiously from her wristwatch to the sea which was already creaming over the rocks on either side of the causeway.

Cilla came towards me, leading my pony, Misty, who whinnied softly in greeting when she saw me.

'Here, Jackie,' Cilla said, handing Misty's reins to me. 'You have a turn. After all, Misty is your pony, and it seems a shame that you've barely had a chance to ride her since we've been at the camp.'

Heather offered Patch to Babs. 'We don't mind cycling back,' she said.

Misty seemed pleased. She rubbed her head against my shoulder as I let down the stirrup leathers a hole, and got ready to mount.

'Hurry, Jackie!' Sheila urged. 'The tide's coming in fast.'

'Carry on,' I called, putting my foot in the stirrup. 'I'm coming.'

Misty was excited. She edged round in a circle, keeping me hopping on one leg as I tried to mount. By the time I was on her back, the campers were crossing the causeway. Hardly had I settled myself when Misty gave a playful buck. I felt the saddle shift under me.

Cilla hadn't tightened the girths. Misty must have used her old trick of blowing herself out when she was saddled, and Cilla, not realizing, hadn't walked her on a few steps and pulled up the girth-fastening another hole or two. By the time I had dismounted and pulled up the girth, the sea was swirling over the first few yards of the causeway. The water was deepening every moment. I reined up Misty, and rode her down the shingle path between the rocks to the causeway which was now fetlock-deep in water.

Not being able to see her foothold, Misty naturally gibbed.

'Go on, Misty.' I drove her forward with my legs. She stopped again. I clapped my heels into her. 'Come on, girl. What's the fuss? You've been in the sea before.'

Sweat broke out on Misty's neck, and she turned a rolling eye towards me. There was only one thing to do. I dismounted and, pulling the reins over her head, led her into the water.

Shivering, Misty hesitated at every step. The water was swirling round my knees as desperately I pulled her on.

'Go back!' called Sheila from the mainland, and I saw the campers gesticulating from the safety of the opposite shore. 'Don't risk it. Stay on the island until the next tide.'

Before I could turn Misty to go back she took another step forward. There must have been a hidden dip in the causeway because suddenly the water was up to my waist. I felt Misty plunge sideways. Hanging tightly to the reins, I was dragged with her, and then we were both in deep water, floundering against the current which was sweeping us away from the shore.

'Don't panic, Jackie,' shouted one of the

twins, and I saw a red-headed figure, in blue jeans, splashing through the water towards us. 'I'm coming.'

Next minute, my feet touched firm sand, and I realized that Misty and I had been swept on to a sandbank. We were safe, but not for long. Soon the racing tide would cover the sandbank and swirl us out to sea.

'Pete!' I gasped, as the red-headed boy struggled chest-deep through the water towards us. 'Thank goodness you've come. How are we going to get Misty ashore?'

By now, my pony and I were standing in the middle of the quickly disappearing sandbank. The red-headed twin scowled as he splashed through the shallows towards us, and my heart sank.

My rescuer was Paul.

'Of all the clots!' Paul groaned. 'Why didn't you go back when we told you?'

I tried to explain, but Paul wouldn't listen. Meanwhile the waves were now lapping right over the sandbank. Soon our temporary refuge would be gone.

'There isn't time for anyone to fetch a boat,' Paul grumbled. 'So there's only one thing to do. Get on to Misty's back and stay there, even if she has to swim.'

With Paul leading her, I rode Misty into the water. From the shore Babs, Pete and some of the others were wading out to encourage her.

'Come on, Misty, old girl!' Babs urged. 'Come here to us.'

Misty's nostrils were flaring as she followed Paul into the deeper water. She was terrified. Then I felt her strike out strongly beneath me while the water reached my knees. My pony was now swimming towards the shore.

'Good girl, Misty.' I patted her neck as she swam. A few more yards and I felt Misty's feet touch firm sand. 'You've made it!'

As we came out of the water everybody crowded round, making a fuss of Misty and congratulating Paul.

'Thanks, Paul,' I said feelingly. 'If it hadn't been for you, Misty would have been drowned.'

'You were terrific, Paul,' said Babs. 'Three cheers.'

'Well done, twin!' praised Pete.

'We were proud of you,' added Sheila.

'For he's a jolly good fellow,' sang one of the boy campers and everyone joined in.

Paul was the hero of the hour and he was actually smiling. For once he and not Pete was in the limelight. I was so glad for Paul's sake.

'Take off Misty's saddle and ride back to camp,' Pete told me. 'That will dry her off and warm her up.'

'And you must change into some dry clothes, Jackie. You too, Paul,' said Sheila. She looked round at the rest of the campers. Everybody was rather wet. 'The sooner we all get back to camp and brew up some hot chocolate the better.'

Back at the camp Sheila insisted on my handing Misty over to Pete to be rubbed down and rugged up while I changed into dry clothes. Then Babs and I hurried to the stables to see how my pony was faring. Misty was looking comfortable, pulling at her hay net, while Pete was rubbing her ears. She whickered as Babs and I entered the loosebox, and I could see that she was enjoying all the fuss.

'Sheila thinks she ought to have some gruel,' Pete said. 'There isn't any linseed soaked, but she could have oatmeal. Will you make the gruel while I see to Magpie?'

A moment later Misty heard Pete talking to the piebald in the other loosebox. Why was Magpie having a fuss? Misty gave a protesting rattle of her water bucket. She hadn't liked being just one of the riding ponies, and now that she was on her own again, and having a fuss with everybody doing things for her, she wanted to keep it that way.

'Don't be such a nuisance,' I told Misty. 'You've got to stay on your own for a little while, and it's no use banging that bucket. Babs and I are going to make your gruel and you'll just have to be patient until it's ready.'

We went to the feed-store. I put a couple of handfuls of oatmeal into a pail, and then took it to the tap and poured out a little cold water, stirring it. Meanwhile Babs went to the kitchen to heat up a gallon and a half of water in several big saucepans.

We were in the kitchen pouring hot water on to the oatmeal when suddenly I began to shiver.

I sat down weakly. 'I do feel peculiar,' I said. 'My legs are trembly.'

'It must be delayed shock,' said Babs, putting her cardigan over my shoulders. 'Sit there quietly while I make a cup of sweet tea. That'll pull you round.'

I put my head in my hands as the memory of my ordeal came back to me. I could feel again the dreadful helplessness when Misty and I were swept away in the water.

'It was terrible,' I said. 'Simply terrible. We might have been drowned and all because

I took such a silly risk, thinking I knew best and that I could get across the causeway in time. I just didn't realize the danger. I didn't know the water would be so deep.'

'It was agonizing for us to watch you,' Babs said in a heartfelt way. 'When Misty was swept into the current, it was all Pete and I could do not to race in after you, but Sheila pulled us back. You see it was Paul who made the first move, while the rest of us were still rooted to the spot with horror. Paul's reactions must have been quicker, and he kicked off his shoes and was dashing into the water before we could move.'

'Somehow I'd expected Pete to be the hero,' I said. 'Not Paul.'

'Well, Pete was going to dash after Paul,' Babs explained. 'Then Sheila grabbed him by the arm, and said: "Leave this to Paul. He'll be able to cope." I suppose she didn't want Paul to be outdone by Pete in everything. She knew that this was something Paul could do.'

'Of course,' I said, taking another sip of tea and feeling better now. 'That explains it. Sheila knew that Paul isn't scared of water, even though he's scared of jumping.'

'Yes,' said Babs. 'Sheila wanted Paul to have a chance to shine at something. In a way,

Jackie, you did Paul a good turn by giving him the chance to rescue you.'

'Did I?'

'You've given him a new self-respect,' said Babs. 'The campers had got fed up with him. They thought he was just a drag, being so bad-tempered, and sulking all the time. Then, when he rescued you, everybody was so relieved that they just rushed forward to cheer and I thought I'd help things along, so I said "Come on, everybody, Paul's a hero. Let's show him that we think so, and then perhaps he won't be such a grouch."'

'Babs – shush!' I warned, too late.

Her words trailed off as she saw the look of dismay on my face. While Babs was speaking, a shadow had fallen across the open doorway of the kitchen.

Paul was standing there.

He must have heard every word. He looked defeated and utterly humiliated. His expression suddenly tightened and he turned away.

'Oh, Paul,' Babs gasped in dismay. 'You weren't meant to hear – it wasn't like that. Really it wasn't. I didn't mean it. Now I've spoiled everything. I'd give anything not to have said it.'

Impulsively she ran after Paul. She grabbed

at his arm. He brushed her aside and strode to the stairs. With Babs hurrying after him he raced up them. I heard a door shut, and then Babs knocking.

I ran after them.

'Paul!' I called outside his bedroom door. 'Come back. It must have sounded horrid, but we didn't mean it like that. We only wanted to help to make you feel better.'

I knocked on the door. There was no reply. I turned the knob. We must talk to Paul. We must straighten things out. We couldn't leave him like this – hurt and humiliated yet again.

'Paul, I'm coming in,' I declared.

I tried to push the door open. It would not budge. Paul must be holding it.

'Please, Paul.' I rattled the knob. 'Let us come in and explain.'

There was a grating noise as the key turned in the door. Paul had locked us out. Babs and I stood helpless, staring at each other in dismay, listening for any sound and hearing nothing. That was what made us feel even worse – the silence.

CHAPTER TEN

MY WORST FEARS

I'll never forget how helpless we felt, staring at that locked door, listening to the silence, and knowing that Paul was on the other side, and so unhappy.

At last we walked away, defeated, and I don't think I've ever been so miserable. Everything, but everything, that Babs and I did seemed to make things worse for Paul. If only Babs hadn't been telling me the truth about the rescue just at the moment when Paul had appeared! What a lesson that was – not to talk about people, especially when there is the slightest risk of their overhearing.

The long day dragged by, and still Paul didn't appear. We didn't blame him for avoiding us. Then, when he didn't turn up for tea, nor come to the sing-song in the barn, I decided that I must try again to make amends. I would have another talk with him. If he snubbed me, well, that was that. At least I would have tried.

I looked around the camp, meadows and farmhouse. There was no sign of Paul. Was he still in his bedroom behind that locked door? I forced myself to go up the stairs.

The door was ajar. He wasn't there.

I hesitated on the landing. Where could Paul be? Had he perhaps again sought solace with Daydream? Would he be sitting on an upturned bucket, talking out his troubles with the pony? I steeled myself to go to the loosebox. Paul wouldn't thank me for intruding. That was sure. But I must do everything possible to try to straighten out the misunderstanding.

As I crossed the yard, I heard a sudden outburst of noise; buckets banging and rattling, a thudding on wood, and the scared whinny of a pony. Forgetting Paul for the moment, I ran into Misty's loosebox, and gazed in dismay at the sight of her overturned feed and drinking buckets and water flowing across the cobbles.

'You naughty pony!' I scolded. 'So you're playing up again, kicking your bucket and banging it. I suppose you must be jealous of Magpie and upset because I haven't been riding you.' I put my arms round her neck. 'Oh, Misty, you're still my pony. When the camp's over we'll be going back home together and everything will be like it always has been. But what made you whinny? Have you hurt yourself?'

I examined Misty's legs for any cut. She was unharmed. Then, from Magpie's box, I heard a trampling of feet and a squeal. Oh dear, yet more pony trouble! I left Misty and dashed into the sick pony's box. The piebald, with his foot through the handle of his feed bucket, was banging it up and down desperately with a dreadful clatter, trying to free himself.

'Magpie,' I sighed, grasping his head and trying to soothe him. 'Just keep still. There! Don't panic or you'll really hurt yourself.'

I managed to get Magpie to trust me. Ears back, he stood trembling while I lifted his fore-foot and removed the bucket.

'I don't know what we're going to do with you and Misty,' I told him. 'You do seem to upset each other. I suppose I'll have to put Misty in the other stable where she won't be able to hear you. It's only for tonight. She's none the worse for her wetting, so she'll be able to go back tomorrow.'

From my pony's loosebox came an indignant whinny. Misty wanted to know why I was spending so much time talking to Magpie. She wanted all the love that was going, every bit of it, all to herself.

'Please be patient, Misty,' I called. 'I'm coming, but there's something else I want to do first.'

Foremost in my mind were thoughts of Paul. Was there a hundred to one chance that he might be in the end loosebox, silently waiting for me to go away?

'Paul?' I called breathlessly as I peered through the dusk into Daydream's box. 'Are you there?'

I stopped in surprise. Paul was not in the loosebox – nor was Daydream! Where was the pony? It was just possible that Pete might have put her in the field with the others. He might have decided to let her have a restful day. I hurried to the field.

In the falling darkness I ran from one sleeping group of ponies to another, checking them all. Pete's mare was not among them. Daydream was missing, and so was Paul.

What did that mean? What ought I to do? Tell Sheila and Pete?

I ran to the barn. The lively music was a contrast to my desperate mood. Sheila was thumping away at the piano, but I managed to corner Pete who had paused in his mouth organ playing to grab a lemonade.

'Not to worry,' Pete said, calmly. 'Paul's probably gone for a ride.'

'You don't understand,' said Babs. 'Paul hasn't just gone for a ride. I think he may have run away. He was upset. Something rather dreadful happened.'

Pete looked serious as we told him everything. He consulted his watch. 'It's a quarter-past nine now. When did you last see him? Six or so?'

I shook my head. 'He wasn't in to tea.'

'No,' agreed Pete, 'he wasn't. But I didn't think anything of it. I suppose I thought that Sheila might have given him his tea in the house as soon as he'd got dry and changed after the rescue. I wonder how long he's been gone?'

'Hey, Pete,' said Cilla who had dashed across the barn. 'The music's nothing without your mouth organ.'

Pete forced a smile, shrugged off his worry and wiped his mouth organ on the sleeve of his pullover. 'Perhaps Paul will turn up any minute,' he told me. 'Don't flap. I'll have a word with Sheila as soon as this number's over.'

Though his tone was light-hearted, I could

see that he was still worried. He put his mouth organ to his lips and began to play.

'Come on, Jackie.' A crinkly-haired boy called Rex came up to me, holding out his hand. 'Dance!'

I tried to throw myself into the spirit of the evening's jollity, although I was sure Pete was now having uneasy feelings about Paul. He was looking anxious. His eyes seemed strained while he played his mouth organ, and I noticed him glancing now and then towards the door as if to check whether his twin had returned. People say that twins can always sense when the other one is in trouble, and Pete was becoming more and more anxious every moment.

Presently he made an excuse to leave the barn, and I guessed that he was going to see if there was any sign of his twin.

Five minutes later he was back. He seemed really worried now. I watched him go across to Sheila.

'Just a moment, Babs,' I said to my cousin with whom I was dancing. 'Something's happening. And I think it's something to do with Paul.'

I pushed my way to Pete and Sheila in time to hear Pete say: 'He's taken his torch, and his sleeping-bag, and the saddle-bags have gone. I suppose he's also taken Daydream's ration of concentrates. I tell you, Sheila, he's running away. I know he is. I can feel it.'

'Paul wouldn't cause us all this worry,' said Sheila. 'Surely he'd have left a note. Perhaps he has, and we haven't found it. We'd better search.'

'Shall I help?' I asked.

'Thanks for the offer, but no,' said Sheila. 'You and Babs go to the kitchen and make some cocoa. It's time the campers were getting to bed. Some of them are going home tomorrow and they've got a long journey ahead of them.'

In the kitchen Babs put on the milk to boil and filled the electric urn with water while I set out the mugs.

I stood on tiptoe by the shelf to reach down the drinking chocolate and biscuit tin. As I did so I noticed a piece of paper lying upside down on the floor at my feet. It must have been propped on the shelf, and then blown down. I picked it up and saw, on the other side, in Paul's handwriting:

Dear Sheila and Pete – You don't need me around. The camp will get by without me, so I'm going to Gran's – Paul.

Babs and I re-read the note, our worst fears confirmed. Paul must have felt that he couldn't face us again, especially after overhearing what Babs had told me she'd said to the other campers after the rescue. Probably he felt that everyone was laughing at him.

'He can't hope to get to his granny's tonight,' Babs said, 'because Sheila was talking about her the other day and she lives at Dorrington.'

'That's twenty miles away,' I said. 'Sooner than wait until tomorrow, Paul set out tonight. That's why he's taken his sleeping-bag. He must have felt that he just couldn't face spending another night in the camp. And it's all our fault. I feel dreadful.'

CHAPTER ELEVEN

IN SUSPENSE

We were in the kitchen, boiling milk for the campers' night-time cocoa, when Sheila telephoned Granny Wayne. The old lady was slightly deaf, which in a way was lucky for us, because she spoke loudly and we could hear almost every word as we stood near the telephone.

'But what's wrong, Sheila?' Granny Wayne asked. 'Of course I don't mind Paul coming here. But he hasn't let me know. I suppose he might have telephoned when I was in the garden and I didn't hear the bell. But surely he's needed at the camp now. He ought to be helping you and Pete.'

Then Sheila told her grandmother what had happened.

'What a pity,' came the old lady's voice, 'just when we wanted everything to go smoothly for Paul, so that he could get his confidence back.'

I winced. The family had been counting on things going right for Paul at the camp; then Babs and I had ruined it all.

We could hear the Waynes' grandmother adding: 'Paul must learn to face up to his problems. Running away won't solve anything. Ah well, I'll ring you tomorrow as soon as he arrives. Try not to worry, dear.'

To add to our problems, tomorrow, Saturday, was change-over day, the busiest day of the week. Everything was rush – rush – rush!

We had to say goodbye to the campers who were departing. We swopped addresses and helped them with their kit. Then, almost immediately, we were welcoming the newcomers. We settled them into their tents and introduced them to each other. Then we asked two of the campers who were still here from the previous week, to take the newcomers to the meadow to meet the ponies, while Babs and I prepared a salad lunch.

Pete and Sheila ate their lunch in the kitchen to be near the telephone, but Babs and I had to take the salad and sliced ham across to the marquee for the hungry campers. After the meal Cilla and Heather and a friendly new boy named Tony offered to do the washing up, so we went with them across to the kitchen to fill their buckets with hot water.

'Any news?' Babs asked as we went indoors.

Pete shook his head, and his blue eyes looked troubled. 'Sheila's just telephoned Gran again. Paul still hasn't arrived. Of course he might have stopped on the way for any number of reasons. Daydream might have cast a shoe. We're going to give him until three o'clock and then, if he still hasn't arrived, we'll have to start searching.'

We had to wait around the camp all day, and so, to keep the campers happy, we arranged some easy jumps in the field. Patch and Bess were jumping in style, and their riders managed to stay on, although Heather was once thrown on to Patch's neck.

With Cilla riding her, Misty cleared the jumps twice before refusing when she saw me watching, as though to say: 'Why have you forsaken me?'

I walked over to the gate where Babs was waiting.

'No need to offer you a penny for your

thoughts, Babs,' I said, seeing how pensive my cousin was looking.

'I can't get Paul out of my mind,' said Babs. She looked at her wristwatch. 'Three o'clock was Sheila's deadline, and now it's five past'

Just then came the reedy sound of a hunting horn – Pete's signal to summon the campers together. Babs looked at me in alarm and said: 'That means there's no news of Paul. This is an emergency. Look, there's Sheila. She's beckoning us to the stable-yard.'

As we reached Sheila and Pete, we could see that they were really worried, although Sheila was trying to keep her voice steady while she briefed the searchers.

'We're going to look for Paul,' she announced. 'Now we'll need some of you to stay behind. Micky, would you be on telephone duty, ready to take any messages? And you, Heather, if you'd stay with him so that you can ride and let us know if any news comes through. Then we'll need two more people to meet the other campers when they arrive and to see that they're fed and settled in.'

'Pam and I will do that,' volunteered a new girl called Gladys.

'That leaves eight of you to search with us, then,' said Sheila. 'Are you all good riders?'

Babs and I looked round at the eight campers. There were Cilla and Wendy and Tony and five of the other newcomers all of whom had handled their ponies competently in the meadow.

'Paul should be somewhere between here and Dorrington,' Sheila told us. 'That's twenty miles away and he may have taken any one of four different routes. There are twelve of us altogether, so we can split into groups of three and each take a different way. Two of you come with me and ride through Sandbeach. Two go with Pete to the Downs Road. Two go with Cilla and follow the route through Low Cross and Minton. Babs and Jackie – take one camper with you and go cross-country. Keep your eyes open all the time, because Paul may have met with an accident.'

'And ask at all the smithies,' put in Pete. 'Just in case Daydream's cast a shoe.'

We collected packets of biscuits and apples from Pete before we mounted. Then, with Tony accompanying us on Bess, Babs and I rode out across the fields, following the bridle path to Marsham in search of Paul.

Misty was overjoyed to have me on her back again, but I couldn't share her joy. All my thoughts were of Paul. Where was he?

Why hadn't he reached his grandmother's? And when we found him – what then? It was obvious that he hadn't wanted any fuss. And now there was the biggest fuss of all – twelve riders out searching for him, tracking him down.

How was Paul going to feel about that? What would he do?

CHAPTER TWELVE

THE OLD WOMAN'S WARNING

'No, miss, I haven't seen hair nor hide of young Paul these last few days,' the blacksmith told us. 'Is anything wrong?'

'We don't know yet,' I explained briefly. Then Tony, Babs and I rode away from the forge through the main street of Marsham village. We turned down a green lane between banks of gorse. Presently the lane widened, and we came to a cottage. Through the open doorway we could glimpse an old woman sewing.

We reined up and Babs called to her: 'Please. can you help us? We're looking for a boy on a bay pony.'

'Would the pony have a black mane and tail?' she asked, coming down the steps.

'That's right,' I nodded.

'And would the boy have red hair?'

'Yes, yes.'

'And he'd be handsome, only he looked so worried.'

'That's Paul,' I said, definitely. 'Please go on.'

'Yes, I've seen him,' the woman declared. 'Last evening. He'll be well on his way by now.'

'Are we on the right track if we ride straight on?' I asked.

The woman nodded.

We turned our ponies, ready to take up the trail again.

'Wait!' the woman called after us. 'He was asking me where he might find somewhere to sleep. I told him there was an old barn about three miles on. To the right of the oak wood, it is. There's no farm near. Nobody there to disturb him. And I gave him some food. Well, I saw the lad were travelling light and I thought he might be needing something seeing he'd such a long way ahead of him.'

'A long way ahead of him?' Babs echoed with foreboding. 'How do you know?'

'Because I told his fortune,' the old woman said wisely. 'Not that there was much fortune in his palm that I could see, leastways not just yet.'

'That wouldn't make him feel any better,' said Tony.

'What else did you see in his palm?' asked Babs.

'Trouble!' said the woman. 'I could see trouble behind him. He was riding with trouble now, and there was trouble ahead. A blight had come into his life.'

Two blights, I thought miserably – Babs and me.

'But it wasn't all fate's doing.' The woman paused. 'Folk's fate isn't all written in the palm of your hand, nor in the stars. A lot of it's what you make it, and mark my words, that lad's at the cross-roads.'

'Oh good,' Tony said. 'Tell us precisely which cross-roads, so that we can gallop there and catch him up.'

'You may scoff, young man.' The old woman seemed to pierce Tony with her dark eyes. 'But heed what I do say. That lad's at the end of his tether, and you need to find him soon. He could go one way or the other, to trouble or to happiness, like the future of the other lad he's linked to.'

Goodness! I thought, suddenly convinced, she must really have sixth sense. She knew Paul was linked to Pete – a twin. Yet nobody had told her. What she was foretelling must be right.

'Where is he now?' I asked eagerly. 'Can't you give us any clue?'

'How can I tell you?' the old woman said. He's not here for me to see his hand. Let me see one of your right hands.' She looked at us in turn and her gaze met mine. 'Yours.'

I wiped my hand on my jeans before holding it out to her. The old woman stared at it for a moment and then said, 'Your fate crosses his by water not by land. That's all I can see.'

We trotted on. When we were out of earshot Tony chuckled scornfully.

'What a lot of rubbish!' he scoffed. 'If any fortune-telling ever does seem to come true, it's either wishful thinking, coincidence or clever guess-work.'

We rode for a little while. Then, sure enough, we came to the oak wood, just where the old woman had said.

At the edge of the wood stood a stone barn in a field of long grass. It seemed a forsaken place; no one would be likely to disturb Paul there. The door lay rotting among a thistle-patch, and dusty sunlight slanted through the doorway, showing up a jumble of hoof-marks on the earth floor.

'Paul must have tied Daydream to this ring bolt,' I said.

'Here's where he made a fire,' said Babs, searching around outside.

We gazed at the blackened circle of the raked-out fire where Paul had cooked a meal. Then we cast around for further clues.

'This is the way he went.' Tony pointed to the flattened grass at the edge of the field where Daydream had passed, girth-high.

We followed Daydream's track through the long grass. We lost it when we came to the next field.

'He could have gone any of three different ways,' said Babs, looking at the public footpath sign which pointed towards Tor Brow on the one side, Brookbank on the other, and Golden Bay in between. 'We'll have to split up.'

'I'll go to Golden Bay,' I volunteered, thinking of the old woman's words: 'Your fate crosses his by water not by land.'

'Meet later at Market Cross,' Babs suggested.

'See you,' I called and split up.

I put Misty over the stile and cantered her along the shady path at the edge of a spinney. We jumped another stile and came on to the downs. Misty tossed her head.

'Thank you for letting me be your pony again,' she seemed to say.

Her hooves thudded joyfully on the thyme-starred turf. Strangely I felt a sixth sense of my own – that we were galloping headlong to something that was written in our fates, Paul's and mine. Good or bad? I didn't know which.

'By water,' the gipsy had said, and there, ahead of me, was the sea shining like molten gold in a V-shaped gap in the hills.

I turned Misty towards the gap, and the breeze rushed past us as we galloped. The path became narrow when we neared the sea. I was eager to press on, but I had to slow Misty to a walk.

We were riding down a shepherd's path to the sand dunes and the marsh. The sea was quite rough, and I could see the darkling shadows of the wind chasing over the water and whipping the waves into white cat's paws. A few hundred yards more and I could see the beach with the seagulls waiting at the tideline. A sense of foreboding came over me again. I shuddered as Misty gave a shrill whinny.

The sun emerged from a cloud, blazing on to the sea, dazzling me. I couldn't see anything. Then, above the cackles of the herring gulls, I heard the thud-thud of hooves on wet sand.

I shielded my eyes, blinked and looked ahead again to see the sun-blurred silhouette of a pony and rider cantering away from a low breakwater. I strained forward in my saddle. Just then a wisp of cloud filtered the glare of the sun at the exact moment that the rider turned his pony.

Now I could see him clearly, his light blue jeans, yellow jersey and ginger hair. I caught my breath, and my hands tightened on Misty's reins.

I had found Paul.

CHAPTER THIRTEEN

FACE TO FACE

Now that I had found him, what should I do? What could I say?

I hadn't a clue. So many times I had done the wrong thing and made matters a hundred times worse. Fervently I wished that Sheila and Pete were here, so that they could cope.

I sat low in the saddle, dreading that Paul might catch sight of me before I had decided what to do.

Then my dread turned to amazement as I watched what Paul was doing.

He was practising jumping. Paul jumping! – yes, the unbelievable was happening before my very eyes.

I crossed my fingers for him to be lucky as he put Daydream into a canter and rode her at the low breakwater. He cleared it easily. It wasn't a particularly high jump, but Paul had flicked the show-jumper with his switch and taken it in style and with confidence. I did so want him to succeed. Suddenly my spirits soared. Paul need not be unhappy any longer. He was conquering his fear. This was wonderful. This must have been his plan, his secret hope, when he said that he wanted to solve his problems in his own way. He must have felt he could only start to jump again if he were far away from people, where no one could see him if he failed.

What should I do? By suddenly appearing on the scene I might spoil everything for him yet again. I decided to ride quietly away, and go to find Sheila and Pete. They might decide it would be best to let Paul carry on working out the solution to his problem in his own way. After all, he wasn't coming to any harm. He'd got the barn to sleep in, and I suppose he had money with him to buy food for himself and Daydream.

I watched, delighted for Paul's sake.

Now he was riding Daydream towards the next breakwater which was slightly higher, though still quite an easy jump. I sat frozen to my saddle so that he wouldn't see me. I would wait until he'd completed the jump. Then he would probably turn Daydream and ride her at the breakwater once more. His back would be turned to me. That would be my chance quietly to ride away. Paul's whole mind was set on the jump. His attitude was one of tense anxiety. His arms were stiff as he put Daydream at the jump.

'Please, Daydream,' I wished. 'Help Paul. Jump for him.'

Then Paul jabbed the pony's mouth. She stumbled on landing, throwing him on to her neck. He slid over her ears and sprawled on to the sand.

At that moment, my pony gave a high-pitched whinny. I suppose she was calling to Daydream, but, to Paul, it must have sounded a mocking sound.

This was dreadful.

I turned to flee. Misty wouldn't go. She was determined to join Daydream on the beach. She dug in her feet, stubbornly stiffened her neck, bucked and then climbed on to a sand dune. Paul scrambled angrily to his feet and glared at us.

'Jackie! What are you doing here?' His astonishment turned to anger and he shouted: 'No. Don't go. I want to know why you're spying on me again.'

My hands quivered on the reins as Paul

flung himself on to Daydream's back, clapped his heels into her sides and galloped straight towards me. I wished the sand would open and swallow me up. Paul reined to a skidding halt, and Misty stretched out her nose to greet Daydream.

I managed a nervous smile. Even that was a mistake. He thought I was laughing at him.

'Yes, very funny. Ha! Ha!' Paul's voice was sarcastic. 'Now you'll have something really amusing to tell Babs and the others. How long have you been watching? Why didn't you let me know you were there? I suppose you were waiting for me to fall off, so that you could have a horse-laugh!'

At last I found my voice.

'I wasn't laughing, Paul. I thought you were doing quite well.'

'Who are you trying to fool? Why, I couldn't even stay on over a two-foot breakwater! I suppose you think I'm such a fool that it was marvellous that I could jump anything at all, even a matchstick.'

'No, Paul, it isn't like that.'

'Isn't it?' Paul was shaking with anger. 'Well, I don't care how it is. I don't care what you think. I'm fed up with you. I was getting on fairly well before you turned up.

Then you had to spoil everything. What are you doing here anyway?'

I gulped. I'd have to tell him the truth.

'I'm one of a search party, Paul,' I explained. 'Everybody's looking for you. Sheila and Pete were worried when you didn't turn up at your gran's.'

'Search party?' Paul groaned. 'I tried to telephone twice, but the line was busy. I was going to telephone again when I rode into the village to get more food.'

'Listen, Paul.' I plucked up my courage. 'Why don't you come back with me to the camp?' I leaned forward to put a hand on Daydream's bridle. 'Everybody will be glad to see you.'

'I dare say.' Paul tried to snatch away the reins. 'Well I'm not coming and you can go back and tell them so. I'm off.'

'Please, Paul – '

'Don't you ever stop interfering?' He faced me. 'You've spoilt the whole camp and the whole summer for me. Just when I'm really trying to tackle things, you have to butt in again and ruin everything. You're a blight, a nuisance and a *pest*!'

I put my hands over my ears to blot out his words. Then suddenly I knew I couldn't take any more. It was now my turn to lose my temper.

'You're the most selfish, thoughtless, stupid boy I've ever met,' I rounded on him. 'You've got a wonderful sister and brother. They try to help you and to cover up for you, and to make a go of the camp, while you're always behaving like a bear with a sore head. You've spoilt things for the campers. You've never pulled your weight. You've only thought about yourself. You're jealous of Pete who's the best and most loyal brother any boy could have. He's worth twenty of you. You're just a millstone round his neck. You're suspicious and sulky. You're always sorry for yourself. You're just impossible. I hate you!'

I broke off, suddenly shocked by my own behaviour and the fact that Paul looked so completely stunned and silenced.

It was as though every word of mine had gone home, and he was realizing, for the first time, how his behaviour must have seemed to other people. He gazed at me, open-mouthed. Then a flush spread over his face. He gathered up Daydream's reins, wheeled her round, and galloped away, too upset to say a word.

What had I done? Now Paul might never again be able to face up to the pony campers not while he thought everybody was thinking horrid things about him.

'Paul,' I called, galloping Misty after him 'I didn't mean what I said. It isn't really like that. Everyone likes you. Everyone's sorry because you're unhappy.'

I broke off. Paul was thundering away, out of earshot.

Soon he reached the downs, and, crouching lower over Daydream's neck, galloping flat out as though he wanted to ride away from everybody and everything.

I urged Misty after him. On we sped over the turf of the downs. Once I lost sight of him when he and Daydream entered a hollow. Then he came into sight, breasting the rise on the other side.

'Paul,' I shouted. 'Please wait.'

If Paul heard, he gave no sign. He rode Daydream even faster, and only once looked back over his shoulder to shout a desperate plea: 'Go back, Jackie. *Leave me alone.*'

CHAPTER FOURTEEN

DISASTER – PLUS PAUL

'Faster, Misty, *faster*!'

I galloped after Paul as though my life depended on it. This time I must succeed in putting things right. It was now or never.

Daydream was well in the lead. With Paul crouched forward in the saddle, she raced up the hill to the top of the downs and then extended herself over the flat turf. Grass flew from beneath her hooves. Her tail streamed in the wind. Twisting between the gorse bushes, she crossed the sheep tracks, plunged down into a hollow and crossed a gulley to thunder up the hill on the far side.

Misty stumbled on some loose stones, throwing me on to her neck. I wriggled back into my saddle, patted her neck and urged her on again. Paul was far ahead of us now. He galloped behind some tall clumps of gorse.

I caught sight of him, twisting and turning Daydream among a patch of stunted thorn bushes. Then he was gone. Just as I thought I'd lost him, I caught sight of him again. He was heading straight for a shut field gate that led off the downs to a lane. He slackened his speed to a canter. This part of the downs was fenced.

'Faster, Misty!' I urged.

Misty was flat out as Paul, not able to face jumping the gate, slid off Daydream's back, opened it, and led her through, pushing the gate shut to check my advantage.

I pressed my heels into Misty's sides and put her at the gate. I knew it was too high for her, yet I had to take the risk. This was my only chance to catch up with Paul and make him understand that I hadn't meant the hateful things I'd said about him, that I'd just lost my temper.

'Up, Misty, *up*!'

The gate was high for Misty, though the ground was firm. She took it gamely, but touched it with her back legs in going over. She pecked on landing, and recovered. Then her back legs crumpled under her.

I jumped off in alarm.

'Misty, what's wrong?'

I bent to examine her. To my horror I saw blood gushing from a gash in her near-hind. There must have been half-hidden wire on the far side of the gate. Misty had caught her leg on it, cutting deeply into her flesh and gashing an artery.

'Paul!' I called desperately. *'Help!'*

Daydream's hoof-beats sounded fainter. Paul either hadn't heard my call for help, or he hadn't heeded it. Blood soaked through my hanky. I tried to wind it round Misty's hind leg above the gash, but it would not reach. It was tiny and useless.

Misty trembled, whinnying with pain. I pressed the blood-soaked hanky as tightly as I could to the wound. Still the blood flowed.

Oh, Paul! I thought desperately. If only you'd heard. If only you'd help. Then I was aware of Daydream's hoof-beats again. This time they were getting nearer.

Paul had heard. He was coming back. He wasn't leaving us in the lurch after all.

I looked up as he scrambled off Daydream.

'Trust you,' he groaned. 'Here, let me.'

He pulled off his belt, and as I soothed Misty, threw aside my blood-stained hanky, made the belt into a tourniquet and wound it round Misty's leg. He tightened it by putting his switch through the knot and twisting it to apply the extra pressure to seal off the severed artery and so stop the bleeding.

'Now, Jackie,' Paul said firmly, 'hold the tourniquet like this to keep up the pressure on the artery.'

'Yes, Paul.'

'Here's my watch. Slacken that tourniquet in twenty minutes. Then tighten it again. Don't forget. It's dangerous to keep it tight for too long. I'm going to try to get the vet.'

I tried to stop my hands shaking as I held the switch. Hoping that Paul would be back before the twenty minutes were over, I watched him mount Daydream and gallop down the green lane.

A gate and stile blocked his way. Paul wavered. He knew that precious moments would be wasted if he stopped to unfasten the gate.

I saw him hesitate for a moment. Then he steeled himself to put his pony at the stile.

Up, Daydream! I prayed.

Daydream jumped like a champion. I saw Paul nearly lose his seat, but he regained it, fumbled for his stirrup and galloped headlong down the lane.

Misty's eyes rolled and she tried to pull

away from me. I held her tightly, took off my jacket and put it across her quarters to stop her shivering.

'Misty, darling,' I murmured soothingly. 'You're the sweetest pony in the world.'

The minutes ticked agonizingly by on Paul's watch. Some sheep bleated on the downs, their lonely cries seeming to emphasize our plight. Misty was standing head down, eyes glazed, dejected. Ten minutes dragged by, then twelve, now fifteen. I watched a jet plane climb high in the sky, leaving a fleecy vapour trail. *Twenty minutes*. With fingers trembling I loosened the tourniquet, only hoping that I would be able to get it tight enough again. Blood spouted from Misty's wound, and I had to force myself not to panic as I waited for circulation to be restored to her leg.

Misty must have felt pain when the sensation crept back into her limb. She flinched and moved, and the bleeding seemed even more alarming. I twisted the tourniquet tight again, holding it there. Misty was uneasy now, and I had difficulty keeping her still.

Hurry, Paul! I prayed, trying to stifle the dread that Paul might be lying injured in a ditch having taken a too-risky jump for Misty's sake.

Then I heard the beat of cantering hooves. They quickened to a gallop, then paused for the take-off. I looked up to see Daydream, with Paul still in the saddle, arching over the stile in a perfect jump.

'The vet's on his way,' he called. He scrambled down from Daydream, tied her to the fence and ran to check Misty's tourniquet. He took the watch from me. 'I've been longer than twenty minutes. You loosened it, didn't you?'

I nodded.

'I rode to the vet's surgery at Little Marsham,' Paul told me. 'He was out on a call. His wife rang the farm that he was visiting, and I told him exactly where you were. He said he would finish treating a sick heifer and then he would come straight here.'

'Oh, Paul, I'll never be able to thank you,' I said fervently. 'You were super. You didn't lose a minute. You jumped that stile as if you never gave it a second thought.'

'I hadn't time to think,' Paul admitted. 'Daydream saw the stile ahead of her, and she just took charge. We were over almost before I knew what had happened. That's how I lost my stirrup.'

'Yes, I noticed,' I said. 'Then you were out of sight. What happened?'

118

'Well, I took another jump. It was only a post-and-rails. Then I put her over the gorse hedge. We jumped on the way back, too.'

I looked keenly at him. 'You know what this means don't you?'

Paul nodded. 'Yes, it seems that I might be getting my nerve back.' His eyes were bright with half-suppressed excitement. 'I shall make myself go on jumping now.'

He soothed Misty, and then glanced up as we heard a car approaching along a bumpy lane. Paul jumped on to a bank, and waved.

'We're over here,' he called to the vet, hurrying to open the gate. A moment later the vet was taking charge, and I knew Misty would be saved, thanks to Paul, the boy whom I said I'd hated.

'I don't want to be a pest, Paul,' I said quietly while the vet was busy with Misty, 'but you must listen for a moment.'

I could almost hear Paul mentally groan. I paused and went on, refusing to be deterred. 'I didn't mean a word of what I said when I was angry. Truly I didn't. None of it.'

Paul didn't answer. He looked down at the ground. I felt worried. Now the emergency about Misty was over, would Paul start disliking me again? Would his former grumpiness return, and would I always go on hating myself for what I had said to him?

I kept my gaze on him. He brushed a gnat from his freckled cheek, scratched his ginger head, looked at me straight in the eyes and sighed.

'You never give up trying, do you, Jackie?'

I shook my head.

'And you know that trouble is always one step behind and one step ahead of you. You realize you're a real jinx, don't you?'

'I suppose so.'

'But then,' said Paul, and suddenly his tone lightened, a smile curved the corners of his lips, and the sunlight was reflected in his blue eyes – 'then if you hadn't been disaster-prone, you wouldn't have got yourself and Misty into this spot of trouble.'

'No, Paul,' I admitted. 'That's true.'

'And I shouldn't have had to ride for help in such a hurry.'

'Go on,' I urged hopefully.

'Then I might never again have jumped anything bigger than that little breakwater.'

'So?' I dared to prompt.

'So if I ever get back into the show ring, it'll be thanks to you, Jackie. That's the truth.'

'You're a sport, Paul.' Warmly I said what I'd really always known at heart: 'A real hundred per cent *sport*.'

CHAPTER FIFTEEN

HAPPY PONY DAYS

Dear Mum and Dad,

I wrote quickly because the daylight was fading, and now only the sunset-glow lit up the inside of the tent.

Nobody will be able to ride Misty for the rest of the camp, but the vet says her leg should heal up all right. He's coming to see her every day.

Poor Misty! She does feel forsaken when the other ponies go out, because she enjoyed the rides and outings so much before she tore her leg. Still, she's getting a lot of extra fuss, and you know how she enjoys that, and she has got Daydream within whinnying distance in the same block of looseboxes. Most of the day she stands with her head over the door,

*watching whatever's going on, and calling
to everybody who goes past.*

*But, just as important, I want to tell you
about Paul.*

I broke off my letter as I thought of Paul. The
old saying: 'To understand all is to forgive all,'
came to my mind. Yes, it was easy to forgive
Paul now that I knew *everything*.

Sheila had at last confided in Babs and
me. I suppose she knew that Paul would
no longer mind our knowing the whole truth.
First Sheila showed me a cutting from the local
newspaper, dated about two years ago. There
was a headline:

DAYDREAM WINS THE DAY FOR
SHOW-JUMPING TWINS

Underneath was a picture of Pete and Paul,
both looking happy and confident, standing on
either side of Daydream. Then there were
the words: *'Paul and Peter Wayne share the
six-year-old mare Daydream, taking it in turns
to enter her for different classes at local shows
and are starting to be successful. Both won a
cup apiece at the Fairfield Show last week.'*

That was the only cup that Paul won because, only three weeks later, he was riding Daydream in some Jumping Trials when the calamity happened. The riders were started in pairs, one a few minutes after the others. Paul had to follow a girl called Ann Adams. The jumps were quite big and the course was twisting, a real cross-country course.

Then Ann Adams fell off at a thick brush hedge, with a ditch on the far side. Her pony was down, too, but Paul didn't see them, and, by an unlucky fluke, the steward's attention was diverted by something else. There was no one to warn Paul. He took the jump and saw the girl lying half-out of the ditch on the far side.

Paul dragged at Daydream's reins, trying to turn her in midair. The mare fell. She rolled on Paul and broke his thigh. It was fractured in two places, and he was in hospital for weeks.

When Paul was off his crutches and ready to try to jump again, he would sit in his saddle as stiff as a toy soldier. His hands trembled on the reins. However, he made himself ride to the jump. Then he'd always pull Daydream aside, and say he just couldn't face it. Sheila and Pete tried to encourage him, but he kept on telling them not to fuss. Paul felt sure he would never jump again. His bitterness became intense. Soon the green-eyed monster, jealousy, reared its horrid head. When the summer came, the other twin, Pete, jumped from triumph to triumph, winning rosettes and cups at almost every show. I could imagine Paul feeling jealous and bitter.

In the end Sheila and Pete decided to put away the cups and rosettes. They never mentioned show-jumping in Paul's presence. It was the taboo subject. They'd decided that Paul must go at his own pace, and they hoped that, if no one made a fuss or badgered him, he might solve his problem in his own way and in his own time.

I picked up my pen again, and switched on my torch because the evening light had almost gone.

And that is what happened, thanks to Fate, and, in a way, to me. I went on writing to Mum and Dad. *Well, at the moment Paul is making haste slowly. He's realized that he isn't ready to jump Daydream yet. He's apt to snatch at her mouth, and of course he doesn't want to risk spoiling her chances for when Pete enters her for the Springfield Show. Paul's still jumping every day. He's practising on Bess who, as it turns out, is just the pony for the job. She's quiet and steady, so that Paul can knot the reins and just hang on to a neck-strap until he gets confidence.*

I think he knows he may never catch up with Pete in the show-jumping ring, and I suppose that's still disappointing for him, but I expect he'll be able to jump as well as most of us. The important thing seems to be that he's made himself overcome his fear and he doesn't feel a coward any more.

Just then I heard running footsteps over the grass outside. Babs's head appeared round the tent flap.

'Come on, Jackie,' my cousin urged. 'Finish your letter tomorrow. Guess who's sent me to find you – Paul.'

Yet another sing-song in the barn . . . I could already hear the wheeze of Pete's mouth-organ, Sheila's tinkle-tankle on the piano, and the twang of an off-tune guitar as we sped through the falling dusk.

Then the thump-thump of a drum was added to the so-called music. When we entered the barn I saw Paul behind a battered drum-set. He smiled across at us, did a thumbs-up sign, and performed a fanfare roll on the drum for our benefit.

'Cheers!' I said to Babs. 'Paul's actually glad to see us.'

A harvest moon shone through the open doorway of the barn, and a white owl flapped across the yard.

One song ended and another was begun. I smiled across at Babs. Yes, this would be something always to remember with happiness after all – our pony camp summer.